SCHOOL
RULES

SIMON & SCHUSTER BOOKS FOR YOUNG READERS
New York   London   Toronto   Sydney

DEDICATIONS

Frindle: For Becky, Charles, Nate, and John

No Talking: For my brother, Matthew Day Clements

SIMON & SCHUSTER BOOKS FOR YOUNG READERS

An imprint of Simon & Schuster Children's Publishing Division

1230 Avenue of the Americas

New York, New York 10020

This book is a work of fiction. Any references to historical events, real people, or real locales are used fictitiously. Other names, characters, places, and incidents are the product of the author's imagination, and any resemblance to actual events or locales or persons, living or dead, is entirely coincidental.

TABLE OF CONTENTS

Nick, age 2 months

Frindle

ANDREW CLEMENTS

PICTURES BY BRIAN SELZNICK

SIMON & SCHUSTER BOOKS FOR YOUNG READERS
NEW YORK · LONDON · TORONTO · SYDNEY

one

Nick

IF YOU ASKED the kids and the teachers at Lincoln Elementary School to make three lists—all the really bad kids, all the really smart kids, and all the really good kids—Nick Allen would not be on any of them. Nick deserved a list all his own, and everyone knew it.

Was Nick a troublemaker? Hard to say. One thing's for sure: Nick Allen had plenty of ideas, and he knew what to do with them.

One time in third grade Nick decided to turn Miss Deaver's room into a tropical island. What kid in New Hampshire isn't ready for a little summer in February? So first he got everyone to make small palm trees out of green and brown construction paper and tape them onto the corners of each desk. Miss Deaver had only been a teacher for about six months, and she was delighted. "That's so *cute*!"

The next day all the girls wore paper flowers in their hair and all the boys wore sunglasses and beach hats. Miss Deaver clapped her hands and said, "It's so *colorful*!"

The day after that Nick turned the classroom thermostat up to about ninety degrees with a little screwdriver he had brought from home. All the kids changed into shorts and T-shirts with no shoes. And when Miss Deaver left the room for a minute, Nick spread about ten cups of fine white sand all over the classroom floor. Miss Deaver was surprised again at just how *creative* her students could be.

But the sand got tracked out into the hallway, where Manny the custodian did not think it was creative at all. And he stomped right down to the office.

The principal followed the trail of sand, and when she arrived, Miss Deaver was teaching the hula to some kids near the front of the room, and a tall, thin, shirtless boy with chestnut hair was just spiking a Nerf volleyball over a net made from six T-shirts tied together.

The third-grade trip to the South Seas ended. Suddenly.

But that didn't stop Nick from trying to liven things up. Lincoln Elementary needed a good jolt once in a while, and Nick was just the guy to deliver it.

About a year later, Nick made the great blackbird discovery. One night he learned on a TV show that red-wing blackbirds give this high-pitched chirp when a hawk or some other danger comes near. Because of the way sound travels, the hunter birds can't tell where the high-pitched chirp is coming from.

The next day during silent reading, Nick glanced at his teacher, and he noticed that Mrs. Avery's nose was curved—kind of like the beak of a hawk. So Nick let out a high, squeaky, blackbird "peep!"

Mrs. Avery jerked her head up from her book and looked around. She couldn't tell who did it, so she just said, "Shhh!" to the whole class.

A minute later Nick did it again, louder. "Peeep!" This time there was a little giggling from the class. But Mrs. Avery pretended not to hear the sound, and about fifteen seconds later she slowly stood up and walked to the back of the classroom.

Without taking his eyes off his book, and without moving at all, Nick put his heart and soul into the highest and most annoying chirp of all: "Peeeeep!"

Mrs. Avery pounced. "Janet Fisk, you stop that this instant!"

Janet, who was sitting four rows away from Nick, promptly turned white, then bright crimson.

"But it wasn't me . . . honest." There was a catch in Janet's voice, as if she might cry.

Mrs. Avery knew she had made a mistake, and she apologized to Janet.

"But someone is asking for big trouble," said Mrs. Avery, looking more like a hawk every second.

Nick kept reading, and he didn't make a peep.

At lunchtime Nick talked to Janet. He felt bad that Mrs. Avery had pounced on her. Janet lived in Nick's neighborhood, and sometimes they played together. She was good at baseball, and she was better at soccer than most of the kids in the whole school, boys or girls. Nick said, "Hey Janet—I'm sorry you got yelled at during reading. It was my fault.

I was the one who made that sound."

"You did?" said Janet. "But how come Mrs. Avery thought it was me?"

So Nick told her about the blackbirds, and Janet thought it was pretty interesting. Then she tried making a peep or two, and Janet's chirps were even higher and squeakier than Nick's. She promised to keep everything a secret.

For the rest of Nick's fourth-grade year, at least once a week, Mrs. Avery heard a loud "peeeep" from somewhere in her classroom—sometimes it was a high-pitched chirp, and sometimes it was a *very* high-pitched chirp.

Mrs. Avery never figured out who was making that sound, and gradually she trained herself to ignore it. But she still looked like a hawk.

To Nick, the whole thing was just one long—and successful—science experiment.

And Janet Fisk enjoyed it, too.

two

Mrs. Granger

FIFTH GRADE WAS different. That was the year to get ready for middle school. Fifth grade meant passing classes. It meant no morning recess. It meant real letter grades on your report cards. But most of all, it meant Mrs. Granger.

There were about one hundred fifty kids in fifth grade. And there were seven fifth-grade teachers: two math, two science, two social studies, but only one language arts teacher. In language arts, Mrs. Granger had a monopoly—and a reputation.

Mrs. Granger lived alone in a tidy little house in the older part of town. She drove an old, pale blue car to school every morning, rain or shine, snow or sleet, hail or wind. She had a perfect attendance record that stretched back farther than anyone could remember.

Her hair was almost white, swept away from her face and up into something like a nest on the back of her head. Unlike some of the younger women teachers, she never wore pants to school. She had two skirt-and-jacket outfits, her gray uniform and her blue uniform, which she always wore over a white shirt with a little cameo pin at the neck. And Mrs. Granger was one of those people who never sweats. It had to be over ninety degrees before she even took off her jacket.

She was small, as teachers go. There were even some fifth graders who were taller. But Mrs. Granger seemed like a giant. It was her eyes that did it. They were dark gray, and if she turned them on full power, they could make you feel like a speck of dust. Her eyes could twinkle and laugh, too, and kids said she could crack really funny jokes. But it wasn't the jokes that made her famous.

Everyone was sure that Mrs. Granger had X-ray vision. Don't even think about chewing a piece of gum within fifty feet of her. If you did, Mrs. Granger would see you and catch you and make you stick the gum onto a bright yellow index card. Then she would safety-pin the card to the front of your shirt, and you'd have to wear it for the rest of the school day. After that, you had to take it home and have your mom or dad sign the card, and bring it back to Mrs. Granger the next day. And it didn't matter to Mrs. Granger if you weren't in fifth grade, because the way she saw it, sooner or later, you would be.

All the kids at Lincoln Elementary School knew that at the end of the line—fifth grade— Mrs. Granger would be the one grading their spelling tests and their reading tests, and worst of all, their vocabulary tests—week after week, month after month.

Every language arts teacher in the world enjoys making kids use the dictionary: "Check your spelling. Check that definition. Check those syllable breaks."

But Mrs. Granger didn't just enjoy the dictionary. She *loved* the dictionary—almost worshipped it. Her weekly vocabulary list was thirty-five words long, sometimes longer.

As if that wasn't bad enough, there was a "Word for the Day" on the blackboard every morning. If you gave yourself a day off and didn't write one down and look it up and learn

Mrs. Granger loved the dictionary

the definition—sooner or later Mrs. Granger would find out, and then, just for you, there would be *two* Words for the Day for a whole week.

Mrs. Granger kept a full set of thirty dictionaries on a shelf at the back of the room. But her pride and joy was one of those huge dictionaries with every word in the universe in it, the kind of book it takes two kids to carry. It sat on its own little table at the front of her classroom, sort of like the altar at the front of a church.

Every graduate of Lincoln Elementary School for the past thirty-five years could remember standing at that table listening to Mrs. Granger's battle cry: "Look it up! That's why we have the dictionary."

Even before the school year started, when it was still the summer before fifth grade for Nick and his friends, Mrs. Granger was already busy. Every parent of every new fifth grader got a letter from her.

Nick's mom read part of it out loud during dinner one night in August.

Every home is expected to have a good dictionary in it so that each student

can do his or her homework properly.
Good spelling and good grammar and
good word skills are essential for
every student. Clear thinking
requires a command of the English
language, and fifth grade is the ideal
time for every girl and boy to acquire
an expanded vocabulary.

And then there was a list of the dictionaries that Mrs. Granger thought would be "acceptable for home study."

Mrs. Allen said, "It's so nice to have a teacher who takes her work this seriously."

Nick groaned and tried to enjoy the rest of his hamburger. But even watermelon for dessert didn't cheer him up much.

Nick had no particular use for the dictionary. He liked words a lot, and he was good at using them. But he figured that he got all the words he needed just by reading, and he read all the time.

When Nick ran into a word he didn't know, he asked his brother or his dad or whoever was handy what it meant, and if they knew, they'd tell him. But not Mrs. Granger. He had heard all about her, and he had seen fifth graders in the library last year, noses stuck in their dictionaries, frantically trying to finish their vocabulary sheets before English class.

It was still a week before school and Nick already felt like fifth grade was going to be a very long year.

three

The Question

THE FIRST DAY of school was always a get-acquainted day. Books were passed out, and there was a lot of chatter. Everyone asked, "What did *you* do over the summer?"

Periods one through six went by very smoothly for Nick.

But then came period seven. Mrs. Granger's class was all business.

The first thing they did was take a vocabulary pretest to see how many of the thirty-five words for the week the kids already knew. *Tremble, circular, orchestra*—the list went on and on. Nick knew most of them.

Then there was a handout about class procedures. After that there was a review paper about cursive writing, and then there was a sample sheet showing how the heading should look on every assignment. No letup for thirty-seven minutes straight.

Nick was an expert at asking the delaying question—also known as the teacher-stopper, or the guaranteed-time-waster. At three minutes before the bell, in that split second between the end of today's class work and the announcement of tomorrow's homework, Nick could launch a question guaranteed to sidetrack the teacher long enough to delay or even wipe out the homework assignment.

Timing was important, but asking the right question—that was the hard part. Questions about stuff in the news, questions about the college the teacher went to, questions about the teacher's favorite book or sport or hobby—Nick knew all the tricks, and he had been very successful in the past.

Here he was in fifth grade, near the end of his very first language arts class with Mrs. Granger, and Nick could feel a homework assignment coming the way a farmer can feel a rainstorm.

Mrs. Granger paused to catch her breath, and Nick's hand shot up. She glanced down at her seating chart, and then up at him. Her sharp gray eyes were not even turned up to half power.

"Yes, Nicholas?"

"Mrs. Granger, you have so many dictionaries in this room, and that huge one especially . . . where did all those words come from? Did they just get copied from other dictionaries? It sure is a big book."

It was a perfect thought-grenade—KaPow!

Several kids smiled, and a few peeked at the clock. Nick was famous for this, and the whole class knew what he was doing.

Unfortunately, so did Mrs. Granger. She hesitated a moment, and gave Nick a smile that was just a little too sweet to be real. Her eyes were the color of a thundercloud.

"Why, what an interesting question, Nicholas. I could talk about that for hours, I bet." She glanced around the classroom. "Do the rest of you want to know, too?" Everyone nodded yes. "Very well then. Nicholas, will you do some research on that subject and give a little oral report to the class? If you find out the answer yourself, it will mean so much more than if I just told you. Please have your report ready for our next class."

Mrs. Granger smiled at him again. Very sweetly. Then it was back to business. "Now, the homework for tomorrow can be found on page twelve of your *Words Alive* book. . . ."

Nick barely heard the assignment. His heart was pounding, and he felt small, very small. He could feel the tops of his ears glowing red. A complete shutdown. An extra assignment. And probably a little black mark next to his name on the seating chart.

Everything he had heard about this teacher was true—don't mess around with The Lone Granger.

word Detective

IT WAS A BEAUTIFUL September afternoon, bright sun, cool breeze, blue sky. But not for Nick.

Nick had to do a little report for the next day. Plus copy out all the definitions for thirty-five words. For Mrs. Granger. This was not the way school was supposed to work. Not for Nick.

There was a rule at Nick's house: Homework First. And that meant right after school. Nick had heard his older brother, James, groan and grumble about this rule for years, right up until he graduated from high school two years ago. And then James wrote home from college after his first semester and said, "My grades are looking great, because when I came here I already knew how to put first things first." That letter was the proof Nick's mom and dad had been

Homework First

looking for. "Homework First" was the law from September to June.

This had never bothered Nick before because he hardly ever had homework. Oh sure, he looked over his spelling words on Thursday nights, and there had been a few short book reports in fourth grade, but other than that, nothing. Up to now, schoolwork never spilled over into his free time. Thanks to Mrs. Granger, those days were gone.

First he looked up the definitions in the brand-new red dictionary that his mom had bought—because Mrs. Granger told her to. It took almost an hour. He could hear a baseball game in John's yard down the street—yelling and shouting, and every few minutes the sharp crack of a bat connecting with a pitch. But he had a report to do. For Mrs. Granger.

Nick looked at the very front of the dictionary. There was an introduction to the book called "Words and Their Origins."

Perfect! Nick thought. It was just what he needed to do his report. It would all be over in a few minutes. Nick could already feel the sun and the breeze on his face as he ran outside to play, homework all done.

Then he read the first sentence from the introduction:

Without question this modern American dictionary is one of the most surprisingly complex and profound documents ever to be created, for it embodies unparalleled etymological detail, reflecting not only superb lexicographic scholarship, but also the dreams and speech and imaginative talents of millions of people over thousands of years—for every person who has ever spoken or written in English has had a hand in its making.

What? Nick scratched his head and read it again. And then again. Not much better. It was sort of like trying to read the ingredients on a shampoo bottle.

He slammed the dictionary shut and walked downstairs.

Nick's family did a lot of reading, so bookshelves covered three of the four walls in the family room. There were two sets of encyclopedias—the black set was for grown-ups, and the red set was for kids. Nick pulled out the

D volume from the red set and looked up *dictionary*. There were three full pages, with headings like Early Dictionaries, Word Detectives, and Dictionaries Today. Not very exciting. But he had to do it, so Nick just plopped down on the couch and read all of it.

And when he was finished with the kids' book, he opened up the black encyclopedia and read most of what it said about dictionaries, too. He understood only about half of what he read.

He leaned back on the couch and covered his eyes with his arm, trying to imagine himself giving a report on all this boring stuff. He'd be lucky to have three minutes worth. But because Nick was Nick, he suddenly had an idea and it brought a grin to his face.

Nick decided that giving this report could actually be fun. He could make it into something special. After all, Mrs. Granger had asked for it.

five

The Report

BY LUNCHTIME the next day, Nick had a bad feeling in the pit of his stomach. Seventh period was coming. He was going to have to stand up in front of Mrs. Granger's class. The eyes of everyone in the class would be glued to his face. And Mrs. Granger's eyes would be cranked up to maximum punch power.

He looked over his notes again and again—the first English dictionary, the growth of the English language, William Shakespeare, words from French and German, new words, old words, new inventions, Anglo-Saxon words, Latin and Greek roots, American English—it all became a big jumble in his mind. And his grand plan from the night before? In the harsh fluorescent light of the school day, it seemed impossible.

What is it with the clocks in school? When you're planning to go to the carnival after school, the clocks in every class practically run backward, and the school day lasts for about three weeks. But if you have to go to the barber or go shopping for clothes after school, zzzzip—the whole day is over before you can blink. And today? After lunch, periods five and six went by in two ticks.

As the seventh-period bell rang, Mrs. Granger walked into the classroom, took four steps to her desk at the side of the room, flipped open her attendance book, glanced out at the class, and made two little check marks. Then looking up at Nick, she said, "I think we have a little report to begin our class today. Nicholas?"

Fifteen seconds into seventh period, and Nick was onstage. *This lady plays for keeps*, thought Nick. He gulped, grabbed his crumpled note cards and his book bag, and walked to the front of the room. He stood next to the giant dictionary on its little table, and Mrs. Granger walked to the back of the classroom and sat primly on a tall stool next to the bookcases. She was wearing her blue uniform.

Taking a deep breath, Nick began. "Well, the

first thing I learned is that the first English dictionary—"

Mrs. Granger interrupted. "Excuse me, Nicholas, but does your report have a title?"

Nick looked blankly at her. "A title? N-no, I didn't make a title."

"Class, please remember to include a title whenever you prepare an oral or written report. Now, please go on, Nicholas," and she smiled and nodded at him.

Nick began again. Looking right at Mrs. Granger he said, "The Dictionary." A couple of kids thought that was funny, but Nick played it straight, and just kept talking. "A lot of people think that the first English dictionary was put together in the 1700s by a man named Samuel Johnson. He lived in London, England. He was real smart, and he wrote a lot of books, and he wanted all the other smart people to have a good dictionary to use, so he made one. But there were other dictionaries before his. The thing that was different about Johnson's dictionary was its size, first of all. He had over forty-three thousand words in it."

The class made a bunch of noise at this big number—"Ooh," and "Wow!" and stuff like that—and Nick lost his concentration. He glanced up at Mrs. Granger, expecting to see those eyes drilling a hole in him. But they weren't. They were almost friendly, in a teacher-y kind of way. She shushed the class and said, "Go on, Nicholas. That's a fine beginning."

Nick almost smiled, but he saw all the kids staring at him, so he gripped his note cards even tighter, and jumped back in.

"The other thing that Samuel Johnson did that was special was to choose the words he thought were most important, and then give lots of examples showing how the words got used by people. For example, he showed how the word *take* could be used in one hundred thirteen different ways. . . ."

Nick's report went on smoothly for twelve minutes. Nick was surprised at how easy it was to stand there and talk about this stuff. At the end of the first five minutes Mrs. Granger had had to stop Nick again to say, "Class, it is not good manners to yawn out loud or to put your heads down on your desks when someone is giving an oral report." No one in the class cared one little bit about the report. Except Mrs. Granger.

Every time Nick glanced up, she was smiling.

And her eyes were not the least bit icy or sharp. She was eating this stuff up, listening, and nodding, and every once in a while she would say, "Very good point" or "Yes, that's exactly right."

But the next time Nick looked up, he saw Mrs. Granger sneaking a look at her watch. Eighteen minutes gone. Maybe his idea was going to work after all. Time for phase two.

Reaching into his book bag, Nick pulled out the red dictionary he had brought from home, the one most of the kids had—the one Mrs. Granger said they should use. Nick said, "This is the dictionary that I use at home for my vocabulary work, and . . . and I opened it up last night to the very front, and right there I found out a lot about how the dictionary was made . . . right in this book. So I thought some of the ideas would be good as part of my report. It says here . . ."

"Nicholas?" Nick looked up. Mrs. Granger got off her tall stool, and its wooden legs made a screech on the linoleum. Heads snapped to attention, and the class was alert again. Mrs. Granger smiled, raised her eyebrows and pointed at her watch. "Nicholas, I think the class should read that at home themselves. Now . . ."

John's hand was up in the air, and at Mrs. Granger's nod he said, "But I don't have that dictionary at home, Mrs. Granger. I have the blue one." And several other kids immediately said, "Me, too."

Mrs. Granger tried not to show that she was annoyed. "Very well, Nick, but it shouldn't take too long. We have other things to do today."

Nick kept his eyes open wide and nodded, adjusted his glasses on his nose, and began to read.

> *Without question this modern American dictionary is one of the most surprisingly complex and profound documents ever to be created, for it embodies unparalleled etymological detail, reflecting not only superb lexicographic scholarship, but also the dreams and speech and imaginative talents of millions of people over thousands of years—for every person who has ever spoken or written in English has had a hand in its making. . . .*

It was a long article, and the kids were bored to death. But no one looked bored at all. Every kid in the room knew now that the period was more than half over, and that Nick's report wasn't just a report. It was one of the greatest time-wasters he had ever invented.

Mrs. Granger knew it, too. She had edged around from the back of the room to the side near the windows. Nick glanced up at her now and then as he read, and each time, Mrs. Granger's eyes clicked up to a new power level. After eight minutes of Nick's best nonstop reading, her eyes were practically burning holes in the chalkboard behind him. There were only ten minutes left in seventh period.

When he took a breath to start a new paragraph, Mrs. Granger cut him off. "That's a fine place to stop, Nicholas. Class, let's all give him a round of applause for his report." The applause didn't last long.

As Nick took his book bag and notes and sat down, Mrs. Granger's eyes went back to almost normal, and she actually smiled at him. "Although your report was a little long—"she paused to let that sink in—"it was quite a good one. And isn't it fascinating that English has more different words than any other language used anywhere in the world?" She pointed at her large dictionary. "That one book contains the definitions of more than four-hundred fifty thousand words. Now, wasn't I right, Nicholas? All this will mean so much more since you learned about it on your own."

Mrs. Granger was beaming at him. Nick sank lower in his chair. This was worse than writing the report, worse than standing up to give it. He was being treated like—like the teacher's pet. And he had the feeling she was doing it on purpose. His reputation was in great danger. So he launched another question.

He raised his hand, and he didn't even wait for Mrs. Granger to call on him. "Yeah, but, you know, I still don't really get the idea of why words all mean different things. Like, who says that d-o-g means the thing that goes 'woof' and wags its tail? Who says so?"

And Mrs. Granger took the bait. "Who says *dog* means dog? You do, Nicholas. You and me and everyone in this class and this school and this town and this state and this country. We all agree. If we lived in France, we would all agree that the right word for that hairy four-legged creature was a different word—*chien*—it sounds like 'shee-en,' but it means what d-o-g means to

Who says dog *means dog?*

you and me. And in Germany they say *hund*, and so on, all around the globe. But if all of us in this room decided to call that creature something else, and if everyone else did, too, then that's what it would be called, and one day it would be written in the dictionary that way. *We* decide what goes in that book." And she pointed at the giant dictionary. And she looked right at Nick. And she smiled again.

Then Mrs. Granger went on, "But of course, that dictionary was worked on by hundreds of very smart people for many years, so as far as we are concerned, that dictionary is the law. Laws can change, of course, but only if they need to. There may be new words that need to be made, but the ones in that book have been put there for good reasons."

Mrs. Granger took a look at the clock, eight minutes left. "Now then, for today you were to have done the exercises beginning on page twelve in your *Words Alive* book. Please get out your papers. Sarah, will you read the first sentence, identify the mistake, and then tell us how you corrected it?"

Mrs. Granger jammed the whole day's work into the last eight minutes, a blur of verbs and nouns and prepositions, and yes, there was another homework assignment.

And Nick didn't try to sidetrack Mrs. G. again. He had slowed her down a little, but had he stopped her? No way.

She was unstoppable . . . at least for today.

six

The Big Idea

THREE THINGS HAPPENED later that same afternoon.

Nick and Janet Fisk had missed the bus because of a school newspaper meeting, so they walked home together. They were seeing who could walk along the curb without falling. It took a lot of concentration, and when Janet stepped off into the street, Nick said, "That's three points for me."

But Janet said, "I didn't fall. I saw something. . . . Look." She bent down and picked up a gold ballpoint pen, the fancy kind.

That was the first thing—Janet finding the pen.

They got back on the curb, and Nick followed Janet, putting one foot carefully in front of the other on the narrow concrete curb.

And while he stepped along, he thought back over the school day, especially about his report. And what Mrs. Granger had said about words at the end of the period finally sank in.

That was the second thing—understanding what Mrs. Granger had said.

She had said, "Who says *dog* means dog? You do, Nicholas."

"You do, Nicholas," he repeated to himself.

I do? Nick thought, still putting one foot in front of the other, following Janet. *What does that mean?* And then Nick remembered something.

When he was about two years old, his mom had bought him one of those unbreakable cassette players and a bunch of sing-along tapes. He had loved them, and he played them over and over and over and over. He would carry the tape and the player to his mother or his big brother or his father and bang them together and say, "Gwagala, gwagala, gwagala," until someone put the cassette in the machine and turned it on.

And for three years, whenever he said "gwagala," his family knew that he wanted to hear those pretty sounds made with voices and instruments. Then when Nick went to preschool, he learned that if he wanted his teacher and the other kids to understand him, he had to use the word *music*. But *gwagala* meant that nice sound to Nick, because Nick said so. Who says *gwagala* means music? "You do, Nicholas."

"No fair!" yelled Janet. They were at the corner of their own street, and Nick had bumped into her, completely absorbed in his thoughts. Janet stumbled off the curb, and the gold pen in her hand clattered onto the street.

"Sorry . . . I didn't mean to, honest," said Nick. "I just wasn't watching. . . . Here . . ." Nick stooped over and picked up the pen and held it out to her. "Here's your . . ."

And that's when the third thing happened.

Nick didn't say "pen." Instead, he said, "Here's your . . . frindle."

"Frindle?" Janet took her pen and looked at him like he was nuts. She wrinkled her nose and said, "What's a *frindle*?"

Nick grinned and said, "You'll find out. See ya later."

It was there at the corner of Spring Street and South Grand Avenue, one block from home on a September afternoon. That's when Nick got the big idea.

The big idea

And by the time he had run down the street and up the steps and through the door and upstairs to his room, it wasn't just a big idea. It was a plan, a whole plan, just begging for Nick to put it into action. And "action" was Nick's middle name.

The next day after school the plan began. Nick walked into the Penny Pantry store and asked the lady behind the counter for a frindle.

She squinted at him. "A what?"

"A frindle, please. A black one," and Nick smiled at her.

She leaned over closer and aimed one ear at him. "You want *what?*"

"A frindle," and this time Nick pointed at the ballpoint pens behind her on the shelf. "A black one, please."

The lady handed Nick the pen. He handed her the 49¢, said "thank you," and left the store.

Six days later Janet stood at the counter of the Penny Pantry. Same store, same lady. John had come in the day before, and Pete the day before that, and Chris the day before that, and Dave the day before that. Janet was the fifth kid that Nick had sent there to ask that woman for a frindle.

And when she asked, the lady reached right for the pens and said, "Blue or black?"

Nick was standing one aisle away at the candy racks, and he was grinning.

Frindle was a real word. It meant *pen*. Who says frindle means pen? "You do, Nicholas."

Half an hour later, a group of serious fifth graders had a meeting in Nick's play room. It was John, Pete, Dave, Chris, and Janet. Add Nick, and that's six kids—six secret agents.

They held up their right hands and read the oath Nick had written out:

> *From this day on and forever, I will never use the word PEN again. Instead, I will use the word FRINDLE, and I will do everything possible so others will, too.*

And all six of them signed the oath—with Nick's frindle.

The plan would work.

Thanks, Mrs. Granger.

seven

word wars

SCHOOL WAS THE PERFECT place to launch a new word, and since this was a major historical event, Nick wanted it to begin in exactly the right class—seventh-period language arts.

Nick raised his hand first thing after the bell rang and said, "Mrs. Granger, I forgot my frindle."

Sitting three rows away, John blurted out, "I have an extra one you can borrow, Nick."

Then John made a big show of looking for something in his backpack. "I think I have an extra frindle, I mean, I told my mom to get me three or four. I'm sure I had an extra frindle in here yesterday, but I must have taken it . . . wait . . . oh yeah, here it is."

And then John made a big show of throwing it over to Nick, and Nick missed it on purpose.

Then he made a big show of finding it.

Mrs. Granger and every kid in the class got the message loud and clear. That black plastic thing that Nick borrowed from John had a funny name . . . a different name . . . a new name—*frindle*.

There was a lot of giggling, but Mrs. Granger turned up the power in her eyes and swept the room into silence. And the rest of the class went by according to plan—her plan.

As everyone was leaving after class, Mrs. Granger said, "Nicholas? I'd like to have . . . a word with you," and she emphasized the word *word*.

Nick's mouth felt dry, and he gulped, but his mind stayed clear. He walked up to her desk. "Yes, Mrs. Granger?"

"It's a funny idea, Nicholas, but I will not have my class disrupted again. Is that clear?" Her eyes were lit up, but it was mostly light, not much heat.

"Idea? What idea?" asked Nick, and he tried to make his eyes as blank as possible.

"You know what I mean, Nicholas. I am talking about the performance that you and John gave at the start of class. I am talking about—this," and she held up her pen, an old maroon fountain pen with a blue cap.

"But I really didn't have a frindle with me," said Nick, amazed at his own bravery. And hiding behind his glasses, Nick kept his eyes wide and blank.

Mrs. Granger's eyes flashed, and then narrowed, and her lips formed a thin, hard line. She was quiet for a few seconds, and then she said, "I see. Very well. Then I guess we have nothing more to discuss today, Nicholas. You may go."

"Thanks, Mrs. Granger," said Nick, and he grabbed his backpack and headed for the door. And when he was just stepping into the hallway, he said, "And I promise I won't ever forget my frindle again. Bye."

eight

Mightier than the Sword

TWO DAYS LATER the photographer came to take class pictures. The fifth-grade picture would be taken last, right after lunch.

That gave Nick and his secret agents plenty of time, and they whispered something into the ear of every fifth grader. All the individual pictures had been taken, and finally it was time for the group picture. Everyone was lined up on the auditorium stage, everyone's hair looked great, and everyone was smiling.

But when the photographer said, "Say cheeese!"—no one did.

Instead, every kid said, "Frindle!" And they held one up for the camera to see.

The photographer was out of film. So that

shot was the only fifth-grade group picture he took. Six of the fifth-grade teachers were not pleased. And Mrs. Granger was furious.

No one had really wanted to make the teachers mad. It was just fun. It also got all the kids in the school talking about the new word. And when people pick up a new word, they say it all the time. The kids at Lincoln Elementary School liked Nick's new word. A lot.

But not Mrs. Granger. The day after the class picture she made an announcement to each of her classes, and she posted a notice on the main bulletin board by the office.

> *Anyone who is heard using the word* frindle *instead of the word* pen *will stay after school and write this sentence one hundred times: I am writing this punishment with a pen.*
>
> —*Mrs. Granger*

But that just made everyone want to use Nick's new word even more. Staying after school with The Lone Granger became a badge of honor. There were kids in her classroom every day after school. It went on like that for a couple of weeks.

One day near the end of seventh period, Mrs. Granger asked Nick to come talk to her after school. "This is not detention, Nicholas. I just want to talk."

Nick was excited. It was kind of like a conference during a war. One side waves a white flag, and the generals come out and talk. General Nicholas Allen. Nick liked the sound of it.

He stuck his head in Mrs. Granger's doorway after school. "You wanted to talk with me?"

"Yes, Nicholas. Please come in and sit down."

When he was settled she looked at him and said, "Don't you think this 'frindle' business has gone far enough? It's just a disruption to the school, don't you think?"

Nick swallowed hard, but he said, "I don't think there's anything wrong with it. It's just fun, and it really is a real word. It's not a bad word, just different. And besides, it's how words really change, isn't it? That's what you said."

Mrs. Granger sighed. "It *is* how a word could be made up brand new, I suppose, but the word *pen?* Should it really be replaced by . . . by that other word? The word *pen* has a long, rich history. It comes from the Latin word for feather, *pinna*. It started to become our word *pen* because quills made from feathers were some of the first writing tools ever made. It's a word that comes from somewhere. It makes *sense*, Nicholas."

"But *frindle* makes just as much sense to me," said Nick. "And after all, didn't somebody just make up the word *pinna*, too?"

That got a spark from Mrs. Granger's eyes, but all she said was, "Then you are not going to stop this?"

And Nick looked right in her eyes and said, "Well, me and . . . I mean, a bunch of my friends and I took an oath about using the word, and we have to keep our promise. And besides, I don't think there's anything wrong with it. I like my word." Nick tried to look brave, like a good general should.

"Very well then. I thought it would end up this way." Mrs. Granger pulled a fat white envelope from her desk drawer and held it up. "This is a letter I have written to you, Nicholas."

Nick held out his hand, thinking she was going to give it to him. But she didn't.

"I am not going to send it to you until all this is over. I want you to sign your name and put

Like a conference during a war

today's date across the back of the envelope. When you read it, whenever that may be, you will know it is the same letter, and that I have not made any changes to it."

"This is weird," Nick said to himself. But to Mrs. Granger he said, "Sure," and he signed his name in his best cursive, and put the date under it.

Then Mrs. Granger stood up abruptly and said, "Then that is all for today, Nicholas. And may the best word win."

There was a frown on her face, but her eyes, her eyes were different—almost happy.

And Nick was halfway down the hall before it hit him—"She likes this war, and she wants to win real bad!"

Walking to school the next day, Pete had a great idea. "How 'bout we see if we can get every kid in the whole fifth grade to go up and ask Mrs. Granger, 'Can I borrow a frindle?'"

"You mean 'Mrs. Granger, *may* I borrow a frindle?'" said Dave. "Got to use good grammar. Don't wanna upset Dangerous Grangerous."

"Sounds good to me," said Nick. "She can't keep everyone after school, can she?"

Almost eighty kids stayed after school with Mrs. Granger that day. They filled her room and spilled out into the hallway. The principal had to stay late to help, and they had to arrange two special late buses to get all the kids home.

And the next day, all the fifth graders did it again, and so did a lot of other students—over two hundred kids.

Parents called to complain. The school bus drivers threatened to go on strike. And then the school board and the superintendent got involved.

And about this time the principal of Lincoln Elementary School paid a little visit to the home of Mr. and Mrs. Allen. She wanted to talk to them about their son. The one in fifth grade. The one named Nick.

nine

Chess

MRS. MARGARET CHATHAM had been principal of Lincoln Elementary School for eighteen years. She knew Mr. and Mrs. Allen, because they had all served together on the building committee when the old Lincoln School was torn down and the new one was built six years ago.

When she telephoned on the afternoon of October first to set up the meeting, Mrs. Chatham had asked Nick to be there, too. It was 6:30 when she knocked, and Nick opened the door.

"Good evening, Nick," she said. No smile.

"Hi, Mrs. Chatham," said Nick, backing away as she filled the doorway. She was a large person, as tall as Nick's dad, with wide shoulders. Nick guessed she would play linebacker on

The game was not over

a football team, because that's what his dad had played in college.

"Hello, Mr. and Mrs. Allen," she said, stepping into the living room. She was wearing a long black raincoat with a red silk scarf tied loosely around her neck. She kept her coat on, but took off the scarf and tucked it into her left pocket. She shook hands stiffly with both of Nick's parents before sitting down on the chair to the left of the couch. Nick's mom and dad sat on the couch, and Nick sat on the rocking chair that faced Mrs. Chatham across the low coffee table.

"This is not an easy visit for me. We are having some trouble at school, and it appears that Nick is in the middle of it."

Then while Nick's parents listened, Mrs. Chatham laid out the story as she saw it—Nick encouraging the other kids to use his new word, Mrs. Granger forbidding it, the ruined fifth-grade class picture, hundreds of kids staying after school, and a general feeling that there was a rebellion at school, with no one respecting the rules anymore.

Nick watched his mom and dad while Mrs. Chatham talked, looking from one face to another. His dad was listening carefully, nodding and frowning. He looked embarrassed about the trouble. But his mom looked—kind of annoyed.

And when Mrs. Chatham finished her story, Nick's mom was the first one to speak. "But doesn't all this seem like a lot of fuss about something pretty silly?"

Nick sat quietly, but in his mind he shouted, *Hurrah for mom, hurrah for mothers everywhere!* His mom wasn't annoyed with him! She was annoyed with Mrs. Granger, maybe even annoyed with Mrs. Chatham. This was getting interesting.

Mrs. Allen was still talking to the principal. "I mean, is there really any harm in the children making up a funny word and saying it? Does there have to be a rule that a word like this may not be used?"

Mrs. Chatham sighed and said, "Yes, I suppose it does seem silly. But Mrs. Granger thinks that it's rather like keeping children from saying 'ain't'—there have to be standards. That's why we have dictionaries. And really, the problem isn't so much the word itself. It's the lack of respect for authority."

Mr. Allen said, "Mrs. Granger's right about

that. There have to be standards. We can't have kids walking around saying 'ain't,' can we?"

And that's when Nick piped in. "You know that big dictionary in Mrs. Granger's room? The word *ain't* is right there in the book. I looked it up, and there it was. I don't see why I can't use a word if it's in the dictionary. Mrs. Granger even said that her big dictionary was the law." Nick looked from face to face to face. That stumped them all. He had just launched a first-class thought-grenade.

"Well, yes . . . but . . . well, as I said, the word *ain't* and even the word *frindle*—these are not the real issue here," said Mrs. Chatham.

Mrs. Allen said, "Well, I think the real issue is Mrs. Granger's reaction to a harmless little experiment with language—it's an overreaction, don't you think so, Tom?" And Mrs. Allen looked at her husband.

It was Mr. Allen's turn to look from face to face to face. He was lost. "Yes, well sure . . . I—I guess so . . . I mean, it's not like anybody's been hurt . . . umm . . . I mean, it's not like vandalism or stealing or something like that . . ." His sentence trailed off, and he rubbed his chin and stared thoughtfully through the window on the wall behind Mrs. Chatham.

And while the three grown-ups sat there in an uncomfortable moment of silence, Nick had a sudden vision of what was really going on here. It was a chess game, Nick against Mrs. Granger. Mrs. Granger had just tried to end the game by using her queen—Mrs. Chatham in her black raincoat, the black queen.

Nick didn't know it until the attack was under way, but he had a powerful defender of his own—good old Mom, the white queen. And the game was not over. It would go on until there was a winner and a loser.

Mrs. Chatham didn't stay much longer. There was a little more talk back and forth across the chessboard about how children have a right to explore new ideas, about the importance of respecting teachers and the work they do, about everybody needing to keep up standards and make school a safe place to learn.

Then Mr. Allen offered Mrs. Chatham some coffee and banana bread, but she said, "No thanks, I really must be going now."

She thanked Nick's parents and they thanked her. Nick opened the door, and said, "Good night, Mrs. Chatham." Then the black queen put on her red scarf and walked off into the October twilight.

"Nick, I think we'd better talk a little more about this," said his mom, sitting back down on the couch. "If I find out that you have been disrespectful to Mrs. Granger or any other teacher at school, then you really will be in big trouble."

"I haven't been disrespectful. Honest. I did get everybody started using my word, but like you said, it's not hurting anybody. And I'm sorry if me and Dave and Pete got everybody to ask Mrs. Granger to borrow a frindle. That was mean, I guess . . . but she started it by making kids stay after school and write a hundred sentences just for saying my word once. All the kids like to use my word. It's just fun, that's all."

"Well," said Nick's dad, "if it gets everyone upset and makes the principal come talk to your mother and me, then it must not be fun for everybody, is it? And I think you should just tell all your friends to knock it off, right now . . . I mean, tomorrow."

Nick shook his head. "I can't, Dad. It won't work. It's a real word now. It used to be just mine, but not anymore. If I knew how to stop it, I think I probably would. But I can't." And Nick looked at both of their faces to see if that idea was sinking in. It was. "Like I said, I won't be disrespectful, but I do like my word. And I guess now we're just going to have to see what happens."

And the chessmen—Nick's king and queen—had to agree.

The game would go on.

Freedom of the Press

JUDY MORGAN WAS a reporter for *The Westfield Gazette*, the local newspaper. Westfield was a quiet little town. There was the occasional burglary, the teenagers got rowdy once in a while, and there was some shouting at the town council or the planning board now and then. But mostly, things were calm and orderly in Westfield, and every Thursday *The Westfield Gazette* proved it.

Ted Bell sold advertisements for the paper, and he had a daughter in fourth grade at Lincoln Elementary. He told Judy that a bunch of fifth graders were making trouble and were not obeying teachers anymore, that there was something about a secret code word they were all using.

And half the students had been kept after school one day last week—including his own little girl.

The only other story Judy was working on was about eighteen new trees that were going to be planted along East Main Street. The trees could wait. This thing at the elementary school sounded like a real story.

So Judy Morgan showed up at Lincoln Elementary School at three o'clock the day after Mrs. Chatham had been to visit Nick's parents. The sign on the door said, "All Visitors Must Report to the Office," and she did.

On the bulletin board outside the office, Judy saw Mrs. Granger's notice about the punishment for using the word *frindle*. She stepped back two paces, aimed her camera at the notice, and snapped a photo. She read the notice once more, and then stepped into the office.

Mrs. Freed, the school secretary, looked up and smiled. "May I help you?"

"Yes, I'm sure you can. My name is Judy Morgan, and I work for *The Westfield Gazette*. I'd like to know about that poster outside the office, the one about this word *frindle*. Who should I talk to?"

Mrs. Freed stopped smiling. She was sick and tired of anything to do with that word. For the past week her phone had been ringing off the hook. If it wasn't a parent complaining about a child who had to stay after school, it was someone from the school board trying to get in touch with Mrs. Chatham or Mrs. Granger. Mrs. Freed pursed her lips and narrowed her eyes. She said, "You'll have to speak with the principal. Let me see if Mrs. Chatham is free."

She was. There isn't a principal alive who won't find the time to talk to someone from the local newspaper. The reporter was invited into Mrs. Chatham's office.

Judy noticed right away that the principal was not comfortable talking about this stuff. When asked about the poster outside the office door, Mrs. Chatham laughed and said, "Oh, that? It's nothing really. Some kids have been playing a prank, and it was time to put a stop to it."

The principal's laugh sounded phony to Judy Morgan. "And did that notice put an end to the prank? I heard that a lot of children were kept after school last week. Would you tell me a little about that? Parents would like to know what's going on."

Mrs. Chatham looked like . . . well, like a kid who had been sent to the principal's office. She squirmed a little in her chair and tried to smile. She said, "Well, we do still have a little problem, but it's under control. Mrs. Granger may have overreacted a bit. I don't think the children have really been trying to be disrespectful. They are just having some fun, and it's more like a difference of opinion . . ." And then Mrs. Chatham went on to tell the reporter what she knew about the word *frindle*, and how it had become popular among the students. Judy Morgan took careful notes.

And when the principal had finished Judy said, "Would you mind if I asked Mrs. Granger a few questions?"

Mrs. Chatham said, "No, not at all." But Judy could tell that the principal wished she would just go away. What could she say, though? Mrs. Chatham couldn't very well keep the reporter away from Mrs. Granger because, after all, America is a free country with a free press. If Judy really wanted to, she would talk to Mrs. Granger sooner or later.

It was sooner. In three minutes Judy Morgan was standing at the doorway of Room

12, looking in at Mrs. Granger. There were about fifteen children sitting at desks scattered around the room, busy writing out their one hundred sentences. She knocked and the teacher and students looked up from their work. "I'm Judy Morgan from *The Westfield Gazette*, Mrs. Granger. May I have a word with you?"

Mrs. Granger stood and came out into the hallway and closed the door. Judy could see past her and saw that every kid in the room was straining to listen. Judy noticed Mrs. Granger's eyes right away—gray, maybe flecked with a little gold, and very sharp, but not hard or mean. Just bright, and strong.

The reporter didn't waste words. "So I hear that you plan to stop the students from using their new word. How goes the battle?"

Mrs. Granger did not smile, and her eyes got even brighter. "First of all, it is not a battle. I am merely helping my students to see that this foolishness should stop. Such a waste of time and thought! There is no reason to invent a new and useless word. They should each learn to use the words we already have. But of course, all of this is just a silly fad, and when you add an *e* to *fad*, you get *fade*.

And I predict that this fad will fade."

Judy looked up from her note pad and asked, "Any idea how it all got started?"

Mrs. Granger's eyes seemed to almost catch on fire at that question, and she said, "Yes, I have a *very* good idea how it all got started. It was one young man's idea, a fifth-grade student named Nicholas Allen. And now you will have to excuse me, Ms. Morgan, for I have papers I must grade." And with a brief, firm handshake, Mrs. Granger ended the interview.

The reporter didn't leave right away. She walked back through the hallway and sat on a bench outside the office so she could look over her notes to make sure they made sense. It took her about five minutes. Then Judy stood up, put her notebook into her large black purse, waved good-bye to a frowning Mrs. Freed, and headed out the door.

As she walked to the parking lot, five or six kids who had just finished writing their sentences for Mrs. Granger came out another door. Judy walked beside them, listening to them laugh and joke. Then she asked them, "Why do you kids keep saying 'frindle'? Don't you hate staying after school?"

A boy who was almost falling over from the weight of his backpack looked up at her and smiled. "It's not so bad. There's always a bunch of my friends there. I've written that sentence six hundred times now."

And then the kids said Mrs. Granger didn't even look at their punishment papers anymore. They were sure, because where you were supposed to write "I am writing this punishment with a pen," everyone was writing the word *frindle* every fourth or fifth sentence. And Mrs. Granger hadn't said anything. One girl bragged that she had written the word *frindle* forty-five times on her sheets today. She grinned and said, "That's a new record."

"And this boy named Nick," Judy asked, "has he had to stay after school, too?"

The kids giggled, and a tall boy with reddish-brown hair and glasses said, "Mrs. Granger has kept Nick after school so much that everyone thinks she wants to adopt him."

The reporter smiled and said, "Do you think I could find Nick and talk to him this afternoon?"

The boy looked at Judy for a second, and then said, "I don't think Nick would want to

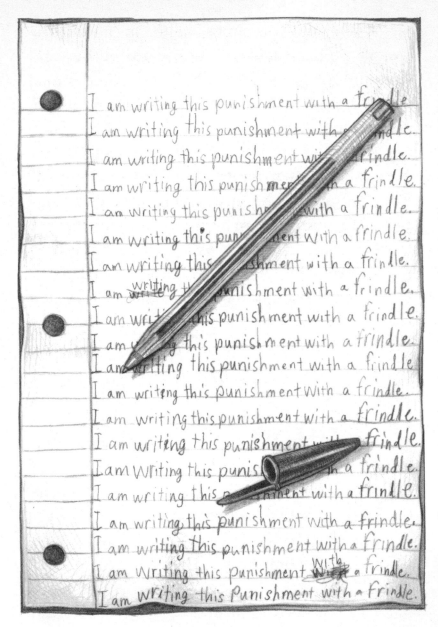

That's a new record

talk to you right now. He might say something stupid and get himself in trouble." Then he grinned at his friends. The kids laughed and poked and punched each other, and headed off down the block. Judy drove back to her office and started writing.

The next morning a brown envelope arrived at the *Gazette* offices addressed to Judy Morgan, and below her name was written "Frindle Story." When Judy opened it, there was a class picture, the fifth grade at Lincoln Elementary School. Mrs. Granger and the six other teachers were standing at the ends of the rows and the kids were dressed neatly, hair all combed. But there was something odd about the picture.

The reporter looked closely and saw that each kid was holding up a pen, and each little mouth was puckered in the same way. She was puzzled for a second, but then she said softly, "Of course! They're all saying 'frindle'!"

Written on the back of the picture in neat cursive was "3rd row, 5th from left."

Judy looked at the picture, and there she saw the same grinning red-haired boy with glasses that she had talked to in the school parking lot yesterday. She chuckled and said, "Well, well, well. Pleased to meet you, Mr. Nicholas Allen."

eleven

Extra! Extra! Read All About It!

ON THURSDAY MORNING, *The Westfield Gazette* was delivered to all 12,297 homes and post office boxes in Westfield. The story about Lincoln Elementary School was the first item on the front page. And the headline?

Local 5th Grader Says, "Move over, Mr. Webster"

It was quite an article. Not that Judy Morgan didn't tell the truth—every statement in the article was completely true. It was the particular way she told the truth that got things hopping around town.

For example, take this sentence about Mrs. Granger: "Mrs. Granger, champion of the forces of order and authority, is battling hundreds of young frindle-fighters. Neither side is giving in."

Or this bit about Nick: "Everyone agrees that Nick Allen masterminded this plot that cleverly raises issues about free speech and academic rules. He is the boy who invented the new word."

Or this last sentence in the article: "One thing is sure: the kids at Lincoln Elementary School love their frindles, and no one seems to be backing off in this war of the words."

And of course *The Westfield Gazette* published the class picture, too. And Mrs. Granger and Nick were identified for all the world to see.

"What is the meaning of this?!" That's what Nick's mother said, putting the article in front of Nick's nose when he got home from school. "Did you talk to this reporter? She seems to know an awful lot about you and your new word, young man!"

"What is the meaning of this?!" That's what the school superintendent said to Mrs. Chatham, slapping a copy of the article onto her desk. "Why did you have to talk to that reporter? Don't we have enough trouble getting the taxpayers to pay for the schools without articles like this banging around town?!"

"What is the meaning of this?!" That's what Mrs. Chatham said to Mrs. Granger, shaking the newspaper in front of her face. "I know you had to talk to that woman, but did you have to say all these things? It'll be a wonder if we don't all get fired!"

It was quite a Thursday for everyone. And no one could figure out how Judy Morgan had gotten that fifth-grade class picture.

twelve

Airwaves

WITHIN A WEEK after the article was published in *The Westfield Gazette*, the kids at the
junior high and the kids at the high school had
stopped using the word *pen* and had started
using the word *frindle*. They loved it.

Nick became sort of a hero for kids all over
town, and he quickly learned that being a
hero—even if you're only a local hero—isn't a
free ride. It has a price.

People noticed Nick when he walked into
his dad's hardware store or when he stood in
line at the Penny Pantry to buy a candy bar. He
could feel it when someone recognized him, and
it made him shy and awkward.

Kids at school started expecting him to be
clever and funny all the time, and even for a kid
as smart as Nick, that was asking a lot. Every

teacher, the office secretary, the principal, even the school nurse and the custodian, all seemed to be watching, always watching.

His parents were great about everything. True, his mom had been upset when the article first came out, and so had his dad. Nick had said, "But I didn't do anything wrong, Mom. And neither did that lady from the newspaper." And his parents could see that he was right. The things in the article were true, and the truth is the truth, and nothing could be done about it now. Even though it made them uncomfortable to have their boy talked about all over town, secretly, Nick's mom and dad were pleased. After all, a brand-new word is a pretty amazing thing. Their Nicholas was quite a fellow—no getting around it.

Someone else in town thought this brand-new word was pretty amazing, too. Bud Lawrence had lived all his life in Westfield, and when he was only nineteen years old, he had saved enough money to make an investment. He looked around for a good idea, and then bought the first Dairy Queen in the state. After a few years he bought a McDonald's restaurant. That was almost thirty years ago, and these two restaurants had made him rich, one of Westfield's leading citizens.

When Bud Lawrence saw the article about the new word, he had his lawyer file a preliminary trademark claim on the word *frindle*. Within four days he had set up a small company that was selling cheap plastic ballpoint pens specially imprinted with the word *frindle*. He sold three thousand *frindles* the first week, and they sold so fast that stores all over Westfield couldn't keep them in stock. Then just as quickly, kids stopped asking for frindles. The sales slowed down, and Bud Lawrence started thinking about other projects.

A week later it was Halloween, the leaves started falling, and it seemed like the town was going to quiet down.

And it would have—if it hadn't been for Alice Lunderson. Alice lived in Betherly, a town seven miles away from Westfield, and she worked part time for the local CBS-TV station in Carrington, a town of about 75,500 people.

When there was important area news—disasters like floods or tornadoes—or sometimes if she came across little stories that seemed cute or original, Alice would call the station news manager in Carrington. If it was a good story or if it was a day when not much else was happening in the world, then the TV station would send out a van with a camera crew to shoot some videotape.

Alice subscribed to all the small-town newspapers in the area to keep up with local events. Most of them were published on Thursday, and they arrived at her house by Monday or Tuesday. Then it took her a day or so to look through them all. On Wednesday morning she finally saw the article in *The Westfield Gazette* about the word war. She read it through twice, and looked carefully at the class photograph. She was sure that this story was a winner.

The TV station manager in Carrington agreed with her. He called the CBS station in Boston, because sometimes Boston picked up stories from the Carrington newsroom. The woman in Boston thought the story had some real zip to it, so she called the network news editor in New York.

When the fax of *The Westfield Gazette* article got to New York, the staff there loved it. They looked over the schedule sheet for the week and decided it would be the perfect closing story for the CBS evening news for the next day, Thursday. Orders flew back through the telephone links from New York to Boston to Carrington to Betherly. By Wednesday at noon, Alice had a "go" order to take the story all the way. It was her first piece to get onto the national news, and twenty million viewers would see it.

Alice Lunderson and her camera crew stood on Mrs. Granger's front porch Wednesday after school. Mrs. Granger was not impressed at all by the lights and the microphones. She looked right into the camera and said, "I have always said that the dictionary is the finest tool ever made for educating young minds, and I still say that. Children need to understand that there are rules about words and language, and that those rules have a history that makes sense. And to pretend that a perfectly good English word can be replaced by a silly made-up word just for the fun of it, well, it's not something I was ready to stand by and watch without a fight."

"And have you lost that fight, Mrs. Granger?" asked the reporter.

Mrs. Granger turned her eyes up to nearly full power as she looked into the camera, and with a pale smile she said, "It's not over yet."

When Alice and the crew showed up at Nick's house, the Allen family was ready for them. Mom and Dad sat on the couch with Nick between them. Nick squinted into the lights. His mom had worked out with Nick what he could say and what he couldn't say. "You remember, young man," she had told him as she combed his hair, "these reporters are just looking for a quick story that will make some excitement. But you have to stay here and live in this town. So mind your Ps and Qs."

As they sat there on the couch, Mrs. Allen had her foot on top of Nick's under the coffee table, and if she pushed down, it meant that the reporter had just asked a question that she was going to answer for him. Mrs. Allen did not trust reporters.

"So tell me, Nick, why did you make up this new word, *frindle?*" asked Alice Lunderson.

Nick gulped and said, "Well, my teacher Mrs. Granger said that all the words in the dictionary were made up by people, and that they mean what they mean because we say they do. So I thought it would be fun to just make up a new word and see if that was true."

"And were you surprised when Mrs. Granger got mad about that?" asked Alice with a smile.

There was a push on Nick's foot and his mother said, "We never felt that Mrs. Granger got angry. When everyone started using the word *frindle*, it just got to be a disruption, that's all. She's really a very fine teacher."

"Yeah," said Nick. "I mean, I learned a lot about words, and without her, I wouldn't have."

"So what's next for you and the new word?" Alice was wrapping it up. She could see that Nick and his parents were not going to be pushed into saying anything controversial. So she just kept it light and happy.

"Well," said Nick, "the funny thing is, even though I invented it, it's not my word anymore. *Frindle* belongs to everyone now, and I guess everyone will figure out what happens together."

Alice also had a short chat with a worried looking Mrs. Chatham, and a smiling Bud Lawrence, maker of the official *frindle*. Then she shot her opening bit and her closing bit, and the camera crew drove back to Carrington to edit all the pieces and put them together into a two-minute news story.

The next night, when all the serious news about wars and oil prices and world food supplies had been talked about on the CBS evening news, the anchorman looked into the camera and smiled.

He said, "It is believed by many that the word *quiz* was made up in 1791 by a Dublin theater manager named Daly. He had bet someone that he could invent a brand-new word in the English language, and he chalked up the letters *q-u-i-z* onto every wall and building in town. The next morning, there it was, and within a week people all over Ireland were wondering what it could mean—and a new word had been created. *Quiz* is the only word in English that was invented by one person for no particular reason—that is until now. Now there is a new word, *frindle*, and here is Alice Lunderson in Westfield, New Hampshire, with the story."

Alice came on the screen with a short introduction. Then, right there on TV, Mrs. Granger and Nick and Bud Lawrence and Nick's mom were talking to twenty million people about frindles.

One of those twenty million people was a producer for the *Late Show with David*

Letterman. And another one of those twenty million people was a staff writer for *People* magazine, and another one was a writer for *3-2-1 Contact* magazine for kids. Dozens of other writers and producers and marketing people saw that story on the news—and all of them smelled a great story.

During the next three weeks every man, woman, and child in America heard about this funny new word that kids were using instead of the word *pen*. And kids in Ohio and Iowa and New York and Texas and California started using it, too.

Bud Lawrence was suddenly flooded with orders for anything with the word *frindle* on it, and he quickly got interested again. But there were complications.

Bud's lawyer said, "You see that stack of orders there? Trouble. That's what that is. We got a trademark filed, but it's only like an application. The whole country knows that that little kid made up the word, and unless you make a deal with his dad, you're going to end up with nothing—maybe even a big fat lawsuit. That kid owns that word."

When Mr. Allen came home at lunchtime,

America heard about this funny new word

his wife told him that he had to call Bud Lawrence. "It's something about the new word."

This was not good news to Tom Allen. He was sick and tired of all the fuss. And being away from the hardware store so much while all this nonsense was happening had put him weeks behind on his paperwork. He'd be lucky now to get his Christmas order in time.

Even though he didn't really want anything to do with it, Bud was an old friend. So on the way back to the store, Nick's dad went to Bud Lawrence's office.

"Tom—good to see you," said Bud. He stood up and walked around his desk to shake hands. "Have a seat." Tom sat down uneasily, and Bud pulled another chair over. "Ever seen Westfield so stirred up about anything in your life? You and Ginny must be pretty proud of . . . that boy of yours." Bud couldn't remember Nick's name.

Tom shifted in his chair and nodded. "Yes, he's quite something, that's for sure. But I tell you, Bud, I'm ready for it all to just die down and blow away—too much fuss."

Instantly, Bud saw how to get what he wanted. "Well, Tom, I'm afraid it's not really going to go away. Looks like something's started up, and people are real interested. You probably saw those bright red ballpoints around town with the word *frindle* on 'em? That was my doing. Just testing the waters. But your boy, he owns that word. I got my lawyer to apply for a trademark a few weeks back, because that's just the way I am. New thing comes along, I like to be right there in the middle of it." He grinned at Tom Allen, and Tom smiled back weakly.

"Right now, I got a shirt printer in Massachusetts and another one in Chicago and another one in Los Angeles making T-shirts with the word *frindle* above a picture of a pen—I mean a frindle. Each supplier has orders so far for over twenty thousand shirts. Profit on every one of those is going to be two, maybe three dollars. And I'm talking with some big pen and pencil companies in Hong Kong and Japan about a deal that could be worth some really big money. They've seen this frindle thing in the media, and they want to buy the rights to the trademark and make a new line of frindles for kids. I'm not kidding—this is a hot, hot idea!"

Bud guessed right. Just the thought of all this made Tom shrink back uncomfortably in his chair. It was way too much fuss.

"Tom, let me be direct with you. As the boy's guardian, you need to do the right thing about all this. I'd like to see where all this is going to go. I'm going to take some risks, spend some money, see what happens. But I need your permission. I need your signature on these trademark papers, and I need to strike a deal with you about permission to use that trademark. I know it seems like a big ruckus about a word, but we just can't tell what's to come of it unless we take some steps." Bud pointed at the papers on his desk. "That's a contract, and it's fair and honest. It gives your boy thirty percent of whatever profits I might make. That's a fair royalty, generous for this kind of deal. So what do you say—make sense? Let me take care of all the fuss, and see if some good doesn't maybe come of it all?" The papers and a pen were there on the desk next to Tom.

He looked at Bud, then reached over, picked up the pen, and signed both copies of the trademark papers and three copies of the contract. "I've got no reason to doubt you one bit, Bud, and I sure don't want to mess with any of this myself. Is that it?" he asked, standing up.

"Not quite, Tom. Here." Then Bud Lawrence

handed Nick's dad a check for $2,250.

"What's this for?"

"That's what I owe Nick for the sales of frindles from the first three weeks," explained Bud with a smile.

Tom looked at the check and said, "This is terrific, Bud, and I'm really glad about it because it'll sure help with Nick's college. But I wish you'd just keep this between us. If Nick knew, he'd probably stop mowing lawns and I'd never get him to save another penny. So just between us, okay?"

Bud said, "Sure, Tom, I understand. Just between us." And they shook hands.

Mr. Allen left Bud's office and walked across the street to the savings bank. He set up a trust account for Nick, and the bank manager said he could make arrangements with Mr. Lawrence so any other money would be deposited automatically. That sounded good to Tom Allen. If he never heard another word about it, that would be fine.

As Nick's dad walked slowly back to the hardware store, he wondered if things were ever going to be the same again in his quiet little town.

thirteen

Ripples

BUT LIFE DID SETTLE back to normal in Westfield. More leaves fell, Thanksgiving came, then the first snow, then Christmas, and more snow. Fall and winter seemed to calm everything down and drive everyone into their own houses.

Things were calmer at Lincoln Elementary School, too. Frindle-mania was over. But that didn't mean the word was gone. Not at all.

All the kids and even some of the teachers used the new word. At first it was on purpose. Then it became a habit, and by the middle of February, *frindle* was just a word, like *door* or *tree* or *hat*. People in Westfield barely noticed it anymore.

But in the rest of the country, things were hopping. Frindle was on the move. In hundreds of little towns and big cities from coast to coast, kids were using the new word, and parents and teachers were trying to stop it. What had happened in Westfield happened over and over and over again.

Bud Lawrence couldn't have been happier. There were frindle shirts and sunglasses and erasers and notebooks and paper and dozens of other items. The new line of frindles imported from Japan were a big hit, and now there was talk of selling them in Japan and Europe, as well. The checks that went into Nick's trust fund got bigger and bigger.

Bud opened his own factory in Westfield to make frindle baseball caps, which created jobs for twenty-two people. And in March the town council voted to put up a little sign on the post below the town's name along Route 302. It said, "Home of the Original Frindle."

And Mrs. Granger? She seemed to have given up, or perhaps she had been ordered to. No one knew. Her poster about the forbidden word had quietly disappeared from the bulletin board, and kids were not staying after school writing sentences anymore. It was business as usual.

Except for one thing.

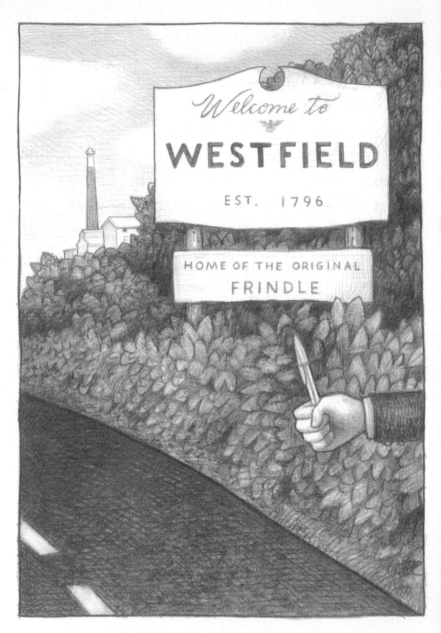

But life did settle back to normal

Everyone in fifth grade got at least one word wrong on his or her spelling test each week. Every week, the first word at the top of Mrs. Granger's list was *pen*. And each Friday during the spelling test, every kid spelled it *f-r-i-n-d-l-e*.

Nick was sort of a celebrity for a while. Everyone had seen him on *The Late Show*, and on *Good Morning, America* and two or three other TV shows. John and Chris and all his friends kept asking about what it was like to ride in a limousine. After a week or two, though, it was old news, and everyone seemed to forget it and move on.

The only person who couldn't quite forget about everything was Nick.

fourteen

Inside Nick

ON THE OUTSIDE, Nick was still Nick. But inside, it was different. Oh sure, he still had a lot of great ideas, but now they scared him a little.

For instance, Nick learned in social studies class that people who buy stuff are called *consumers*. If consumers stop buying, stores and shops and restaurants go out of business.

Then—boom—a new idea hit him.

All the kids loved lunchtime. But the awful part about lunch was the eating part—school food. And the food was never a surprise—you had to smell it all morning and then go eat it. The food was always bad.

Well, thought Nick, *the school cafeteria is sort of a restaurant, isn't it? And the students are the consumers, right? And we don't really have to buy our lunches there, do we?*

Nick could see it all: He would get all the kids to bring their lunches from home every day until the ladies who made the lunches cooked better food. He was sure those women didn't cook food like that for their own families. The kids were the consumers with $1.35 in their pockets, and until the food was better, that's where their money would stay.

Great idea! Nick was sure it would work, and he got all excited about it.

But then Nick remembered what had happened with *frindle*. It stopped him cold. He was sure that if all the kids stopped buying lunch, sooner or later someone would figure out that it was all Nick Allen's idea. He would get in trouble. People would write about it in the newspaper. The principal would call his parents— anything could happen.

So for the first time in his life, Nick kept a good idea to himself. He never even told John or Chris.

And that changed Nick.

His mom was the first to notice. "Are things okay at school, honey?" she asked one day in early March. He had seemed kind of down, a little sad. It worried her.

"Sure," said Nick. "Everything's fine."

"Everything's okay with your friends? They haven't been hanging around here very much."

"Mom, honest. Everything's fine. It's winter. Everyone's really busy with hockey and basketball—that's all." And Nick went to his room and shut the door.

Mrs. Granger noticed the change, too. The clever little rascal who had looked her in the eye and said, "But I really didn't have a frindle with me—" that boy wasn't in her class anymore. Now a quieter, more careful Nicholas Allen came into class every day. He did all his work perfectly, didn't speak unless she called on him, and didn't laugh and joke with his friends like he used to. School would be over in a few months, and it seemed like there was nothing she could do to help him.

Toward the end of the year, Nick remembered the letter that Mrs. Granger had asked him to sign on the back when the frindle business was just getting started. The chess game was over, so he was expecting to get that letter from Mrs. Granger any day. But all spring it didn't come, so he thought she must have forgotten about it. Nick was afraid to bring it all up again, but he was dying of curiosity.

So on the last day of school, Nick knocked on Mrs. Granger's classroom door. She was straightening up the textbooks on the bookcases below the windows. Without turning around she sang out, "Come in."

Nick said, "Hi, Mrs. Granger."

Mrs. Granger stood up and turned to face him. "Oh, it's you, Nicholas. I'm so glad you stopped by. I've been meaning to talk to you, and this will save me having to send you a letter this summer."

Nick gulped and said, "That's what I came for—the letter."

Mrs. Granger looked puzzled for half a second, and then she said, "Oh! That letter." Then she paused. "You will recall, Nicholas, that I said I would send you that letter when all this was over . . . and it's not over."

"It's not?" Nick tilted his head to one side, and asked, "When will it be over?"

Mrs. Granger smiled and said, "Oh, believe me, Nicholas. You'll know when it's over. I wanted to talk to you about something else."

She walked across the room and stood about two feet from him. Nick had grown during the year, and their eyes were almost on the same level. Nick noticed that the eyes were softer, but just as powerful. "I've noticed that you've been very quiet for the past few months. You know, Nicholas, you didn't do anything wrong this year. I know a lot of things happened, and a lot of things were said, and you must have had some difficult days here and there. But your idea was a good idea, and I have been very proud of the way you behaved—most of the time."

Nick was embarrassed, but Mrs. Granger kept on talking. "And Nicholas, you have great things to do in this life. I'm absolutely sure you do, and you mustn't let a few hard days trick you into clamming up."

Then Mrs. Granger reached out and shook Nick's hand, and looked him in the face. Her eyes were turned up brighter than Nick had ever seen them before. She said, "Nicholas Allen, I have enjoyed having you as a student. Now you go out there and have a wonderful summer. And I expect to hear remarkable things about you, young man. "

Mrs. Granger watched Nick start to leave. But before he got to the door, he turned and said, "Thanks, Mrs. Granger. You have a great summer, too." Then he grinned and said, "And don't forget to buy some new frindles for next year."

Thanks to his little talk with Mrs. Granger—along with a healthy dose of summer vacation—Nick made a full recovery. He was proud that he had made up a new word, and he enjoyed thinking about all the commotion it had stirred up. That one little word had made fifth grade a year to remember.

Before he started sixth grade Nick was Nick again, and all through junior high and high school and college, he proved it.

For example, two years later, all the school cafeterias in town were serving delicious food at least four days a week, all because of Nick the Consumer. And the state superintendent of schools had made a special trip to Westfield to learn why this little town had the most success-ful school lunch program in the state.

And in high school, well, the stories about Nick's other adventures could go on and on and on. But that would delay the end of this story, the one that started when Nick was in fifth grade.

Because the end of this story came later—ten years later.

And what was happening to Nick's word during those ten years? Nothing fancy, nothing exciting. Words don't work that way. Words either get used, or they don't. And *frindle* was being used more and more. It was becoming a real word.

fifteen

And the winner Is . . .

TEN YEARS LATER, Nick Allen was a junior in college. And during November of his junior year, two important things happened.

First, Nick turned twenty-one years old, and the frindle trust fund set up by his father became legally Nick's.

Nick was rich. Nick was very rich. Nick was so rich he couldn't even begin to imagine how rich he really was.

Nick wanted to give his parents some of the money, which they said they did *not* need and would *not* accept. But Nick reminded them that they had always wanted to travel, and they should just think of this as a big birthday present or something. So they accepted.

And Nick also wanted to give some money to his big brother, James—who said he did *not* need it and would *not* accept it. But Nick reminded James that his two-year-old daughter would grow up and go to college someday—and besides, hadn't James once given Nick his whole baseball card collection? So James accepted the gift.

After that Nick went out and bought himself a fast new computer. And about ten new games. And a mountain bike. Then he tried to forget about the money, which is a hard thing to do. But he managed pretty well and kept working on his college degree as hard as ever.

The second important thing that fall was the arrival of a package at the door of Nick's apartment one day—a large, heavy package. It was from Mrs. Granger.

There were three things in the package: 1) a brand-new eighth-edition *Webster's College Dictionary*; 2) a short handwritten note taped to the cover of the dictionary; and 3) a fat white envelope. Turning the white envelope over, Nick saw the name—his name. He had written it there one September afternoon in Mrs. Granger's room after school. Ten years ago.

Nick set the envelope down and gently peeled the note off the front of the dictionary.

My dear Nicholas:

Please turn to page 541 of this book.

Nick grabbed the dictionary and leafed to page 541, his heart pounding. And there between *Friml* and *fringe* he read:

> **frin•dle** *(frin' dl)* **n.** *a device used to write or make marks with ink [arbitrary coinage; originated by Nicholas Allen, American, 1987– (see **pen**)]*

Nick went back to the note from Mrs. Granger.

> *This is a brand-new dictionary, the one I recommend that my students use for their homework. And now when I teach them how new words are added to the dictionary, I tell each and every one of them to look up the word frindle.*

> *And, of course, I have sent along that letter I promised to give you when our little battle was over.*

> *And now it's over.*

Your teacher,

Mrs. Lorelei Granger

Nick's head was spinning. With shaking hands, he opened the fat white envelope. He pulled out the ten-year-old letter and began to read.

Dear Nicholas:

If you are reading this letter, it means that the word frindle *has been added to the dictionary. Congratulations.*

A person can watch the sunrise, but he cannot slow it down or stop it or make it go backward. And that is what I was trying to do with your word.

At first I was angry. I admit that. I was not happy to see the word pen *pushed aside as if it did not matter. But I guess that if the Latin word for feather had been* frindilus *instead of* pinna, *then you probably would have invented the word* pen *instead. Like the sunrise, some things just have to happen—and all you can really do is watch.*

The word frindle *has existed for less than three weeks. I now see that this is the kind of chance that a teacher hopes for and dreams about—a chance to see bright young students take an idea they have learned in a boring old classroom and put it to a real test in their own world. I confess that I am very excited to see how it all turns out. I am mostly here to watch it happen.*

But somehow I think I have a small part to play in this drama, and I have chosen to be the villain. Every good story needs a bad guy, don't you think?

So someday, I will be asking you to forgive me, and I hope you will.

Nick, I know you like to think. Please think about this: When I started teaching, no one had landed on the moon, there were no space shuttles, no CNN, no weather satellites. There were no video cassette recorders, no CDs, no computers.

The world has changed in a million

ways. That is why I have always tried to teach children something that would be useful no matter what.

So many things have gone out of date. But after all these years, words are still important. Words are still needed by everyone. Words are used to think with, to write with, to dream with, to hope and pray with. And that is why I love the dictionary. It endures. It works. And as you now know, it also changes and grows.

Again, congratulations. And I've enclosed a little present for you.

Yours truly,

Mrs. Granger

Nick remembered Mrs. Granger's eyes, and now he understood what some of those special looks had meant. The old fox! She had been rooting for *frindle* the whole time. By fighting against it, she had actually helped it along.

There was a flat, oblong case in the white

envelope, the kind of case you get when you buy a watch. Nick pulled it out and opened the lid. Inside was something else Nick had not seen for ten years. It was Mrs. Granger's favorite pen, her old maroon fountain pen with the blue cap. And under the clip was a little folded piece of paper. It was another note. A very short note. Just one word: Frindle.

About a month later, something happened over in the old part of Westfield, over where the trees are huge and the houses are small. On Christmas morning, Mrs. Granger's doorbell rang. Mrs. Granger opened the door, but no one was there.

Someone had left a package inside her storm door—a box wrapped in green paper with a red bow and a white envelope taped to one end. She smiled as she stooped down to pick it up.

As she picked up the package she noticed a red, white, and blue Express Mail envelope sticking halfway out of her mailbox next to the doorway. It must have been delivered late on Christmas Eve. She opened the storm door plucked the envelope from the mailbox, and

FRINDLE

then shut both doors and went inside with a shiver.

Mrs. Granger went across the living room and sat on the couch. The express envelope was from the Westfield School District office. It looked important, so Mrs. Granger opened it right away.

It was a letter from the superintendent of schools, a letter of congratulations. A permanent trust fund for college scholarships had been established with a donation of one million dollars "from one of your former students."

It would be called The Lorelei Granger Students' Fund.

Mrs. Granger was sure it was a mistake. Or maybe a prank. A million dollars? Nonsense! She had the urge to pick up the telephone and give the superintendent a call and straighten this out right away.

But this was Christmas morning, and even though the superintendent *was* one of her former pupils, Mrs. Granger decided to wait a day. Couldn't hurt.

Besides, the other package was sitting next to her on the couch, waiting impatiently with its red bow. She opened the envelope first.

It was a little Christmas card with a sloppy note—obviously the work of a fifth-grade boy.

Dear Mrs. Granger;

Your one of my favorite teachers. Here is somthing I want you to have.

Sincerly,

A student of yours

Mrs. Granger glared at the spelling mistakes, but then chuckled and shook her head. Kids are always the same, year after year. Here she was in her forty-fifth year of teaching, all set to retire in June. She could hardly remember a Christmas day when she didn't have a present from one of her students.

Mrs. Granger pulled off the red ribbon and tore off the paper and lifted the lid of the box. She expected to find something made of yarn and popsicle sticks, or maybe curly macaroni and glue.

But instead she found an oblong case covered with blue velvet. She opened the case and inside was a beautiful gold fountain pen. She picked it up, and it was cool and heavy in her hand. Words were engraved along the pen's shiny barrel, and Mrs. Granger had to slide down to the end of the couch and turn on her reading lamp. Then she could read the three thin lines of type:

This object belongs to Mrs. Lorelei Granger, and she may call it any name she chooses.
                    —With love from Nicholas Allen

Andrew Clements

Illustrations by Mark Elliott

Simon & Schuster Books for Young Readers

New York · London · Toronto · Sydney

CHAPTER 1

ZIPPED

Dave Packer was in the middle of his fourth hour of not talking. He was also in the middle of his social studies class on a Monday morning in the middle of November. And Laketon Elementary School was in the middle of a medium-size town in the middle of New Jersey.

There was a reason Dave was in the middle of his fourth hour of not talking, but this isn't the time to tell about that. This is the time to tell what he figured out in the middle of his social studies class.

Dave figured out that not talking is *extra* hard at school. And the reason? Teachers. Because at 11:35 Mrs. Overby clapped her hands and said, "Class— class! Quiet down!" Then she looked at her list and said, "Dave and Lynsey, you're next."

So Dave nodded at Lynsey and stood up. It was time to present their report about India.

109

But giving this report would ruin his experiment. Because Dave was trying to keep his mouth shut all day. He wanted to keep his lips zipped right up to the very end of the day, to not say one single word until the last bell rang at ten after three. And the reason Dave had decided to clam up . . . but it still isn't the time to tell about that. This is the time to tell what he did about the report.

Dave and Lynsey walked to the front of the room. Dave was supposed to begin the presentation by telling about the history of India. He looked down at his index cards, looked up at Mrs. Overby, looked out at the class, and he opened his mouth.

But he didn't talk.

He coughed. Dave coughed for about ten seconds. Then he wiped his mouth, looked at his index cards again, looked at Mrs. Overby again, looked at the class again, opened his mouth again, and . . . coughed some more. He coughed and coughed and coughed until his face was bright red and he was all bent over.

Lynsey stood there, feeling helpless. Dave hadn't told her about his experiment, so all she could do was watch—and listen to his horrible coughing. Lynsey's opinion of Dave had never been high, and it sank lower by the second.

Mrs. Overby thought she knew what was happening with Dave. She had seen this before—kids who got so nervous that they made themselves sick rather than talk in front of the class. It surprised her, because Dave wasn't shy at all. Ever. In fact, *none* of this year's fifth graders were the least bit shy or nervous about talking. Ever.

But the teacher took pity, and she said, "You'd better go get some water. You two can give your report later."

Lynsey gave Dave a disgusted look and went back to her desk.

Dave nodded at Mrs. Overby, coughed a few more times for good measure, and hurried out of the room.

And with Dave out in the hall getting a drink, it's the perfect time to tell why he was in the middle of his fourth hour of not talking, and why he had decided to keep quiet in the first place.

CHAPTER 2

GANDHI

When something happens, there's usually a simple explanation. But that simple explanation is almost never the full story.

Here's the simple explanation anyway: Dave had decided to stop talking for a whole day because of something he'd read in a book.

See? Very simple, very clear. But it's not the whole story.

So here's a little more.

Dave and a partner had to prepare a report on India—not a long one, just some basic facts. Something about the history, something about the government, something about the land and the industry, something about the Indian people and their culture. Five minutes or less.

Dave's report partner was Lynsey Burgess, and neither one of them was happy about that—there were some boy-girl problems at Laketon Elementary School. But this isn't the time to tell about that.

Even though Dave and Lynsey had to *give* their report together, they both agreed that they did *not* want to *prepare* it together. So they divided the topics in half, and each worked alone.

Dave was a good student, and he had found two books about India, and he had checked them out of the library. He hadn't read both books, not completely—he wasn't *that* good a student. But he had read parts of both books.

Dave thought the most interesting section in each book was the part about how India became independent, how the country broke away from England to become a free nation—sort of like the United States did.

And Dave thought the most interesting person in the story of India's independence was Mahatma Gandhi.

Dave was amazed by Gandhi. This one skinny little man practically pushed the whole British army out of India all by himself. But he didn't use weapons or violence. He fought with words and ideas. It was an incredible story, all of it true.

And in one of the books, Dave read this about Gandhi:

> For many years, one day each week
> Gandhi did not speak at all. Gandhi
> believed this was a way to bring
> order to his mind.

Dave read that bit of information on Thursday afternoon, and he read it again on Sunday night as he prepared for his oral report. And it made him wonder what that would be like—to go a whole day without saying a single word. And Dave began to wonder if not talking would bring order to *his* mind too.

In fact, Dave wondered what that meant, "to bring order to his mind." Could something as simple as not talking change the way your mind worked? Seemed like it must have been good for Gandhi. But what would it do for a regular kid in New Jersey?

Would not talking make him . . . smarter? Would he finally understand fractions? If he had more order in his mind, would he be able to look at a sentence and *see* which word was an adverb—instead of just guessing? And how about sports? Would someone with a more orderly mind be a better baseball player?

Powerful questions.

So Dave decided to zip his lip and give it a try.

Was it hard for him to keep quiet? You bet, especially at first, like when he got to the bus stop, where his friends were arguing about why the Jets had lost to the Patriots. But Dave had learned quickly that by nodding and smiling, by frowning and shrugging, by shaking his head, by giving a thumbs-up or a high five, or even by just putting his hands in his coat pockets and turning away, not talking was possible. And by the time he'd ridden the bus to school, Dave had gotten pretty good at fitting in without speaking up.

There. That explains what's going on a little better. And it's probably enough, at least for the moment. But there's more. There's *always* more.

And now we're back in class on Monday with Dave, who got through the rest of social studies without saying a word. And when the bell rang at the end of the period, it was time for fifth-grade lunch.

More than a hundred and twenty-five kids began hurrying toward the cafeteria. And by the time they got there, the fifth graders were already talking like crazy—all except one.

CHAPTER 3

INSULTS

"If you had to shut up for five minutes, I bet the whole top of your head would explode!" As those words flew out of his mouth, Dave had two thoughts.

First, he thought, *Darn it!*—because he remembered he'd been trying not to talk at all.

And his second thought was, *Gandhi probably wouldn't have said that*. Because it wasn't a very nice thing to say.

But that's what Dave said, and he said it to Lynsey Burgess, and there was a reason he said it.

So it's time to back up a little and explain.

Dave had gotten through the lunch line without a peep. He had pointed at the pizza plate, then pointed at the fruit cup. He had nodded for "yes, please" and shook his head for "no, thanks." He had grabbed some milk from the cooler and flashed his lunch pass at Mrs. Vitelli. And he had smiled a lot.

No talking? No problem.

Then he'd sat down at a table with some of his friends, just like always. But instead of jumping into the conversation, Dave had kept a pleasant look on his face, and he'd kept his mouth full of food.

No talking? No problem.

And because he wasn't talking, Dave had focused all his energy on listening.

Listening at the lunch table, really *listening*, was a brand-new experience for him. Because most of the time Dave was a loudmouth.

See? There's something more about Dave. And it makes Dave's reaction to Gandhi make more sense. Because if Dave himself was a loudmouth, a real tongue-flapper, then someone like Gandhi who could keep completely quiet would seem that much more amazing.

Because Dave really did love to talk. He could talk and talk and talk about almost anything—baseball, cars, dinosaurs, rock hunting, soccer, snowboarding, waterskiing, favorite books, best football players, camping, canoeing, PlayStation, Nintendo, Xbox, comic books, TV shows, movies—you name it. Dave had a long, long list of interests, and he had plenty of opinions.

Plus, talking always made Dave feel like he was in charge. It was sort of like being a police officer out in the middle of traffic. As long as *he* did the talking, the traffic went the way *he* wanted it to. This was especially useful if insults started flying around. When it came to dishing out the put-downs, Dave was a pro.

But this lunchtime, all the *other* loudmouths were getting a chance to spout off.

So Dave had chewed his pizza, and sipped his milk, and listened. And after a minute or two he began listening to Lynsey Burgess. But only because he couldn't help it.

Even though she was sitting behind him at the next table, and even though the cafeteria was almost bursting with noise, Lynsey had a sharp voice, the kind that cuts like a hacksaw.

". . . so I said, 'Are you serious?' and she said, 'What's wrong with you?' and I said, 'Because I saw it first,' and I did, and it was a great color for me, because my hair's brown, and her hair's that mousy blond color, but her mom was right there in the store, so she picked it up and took it over to her, and her mom bought it! Can you *believe* that? She *knew* I wanted that sweater more than anything, and she bought it anyway. And then? After school on Friday at soccer practice? She *smiled* at me, like she wanted to be friends or something—as *if*! Can you *believe* that?"

No, Dave couldn't believe it. He couldn't believe that anyone could flap and yap her mouth so fast, and say so many words, and be so boring and stupid-sounding, all at the same time. He took another bite of pizza and tried to stop listening, but Lynsey was just getting warmed up.

". . . because then, she comes over *after* practice? And she says, 'Here, this is for you,' and she tries to *give* me the sweater. So I pull my hands away like she's holding a dead skunk or something, and I say, 'You think I want *that*? That thing is so ugly, I would *never* wear that!' And she says, 'Oh'—just like that—just, 'Oh'—and she walks away with the sweater. Except now, I wish I hadn't said that, because it really is the *best* color, and it's really soft. . . ."

By this point, Dave was wishing he had an iPod. Because if he had one, and if it hadn't been against school rules, he could have plugged up both his ears and cranked the volume. Anything to get away from the sound of Lynsey's voice.

". . . because once I tried wearing this sweater that was made of wool? And it made my neck itch *so* much, like, I couldn't even wear it for two minutes, but it was okay, because then my mom found this turtleneck way down in the bottom of my dresser, and I'd forgotten I even had it, and it was pink, so then I put that on first, and then the sweater was fine, because, really, it was like the two colors went together *perfectly*, almost like a picture in a magazine. Because last week in *Teen People*? Jenna and Lori and Keith were at this party, like, in Hollywood or somewhere? And Jenna had on a sweater that was almost like that wool one I have, and she was wearing these . . ."

And that was the moment when Dave completely forgot about keeping silent, and he turned around and almost shouted, "If you had to shut up for five minutes, I bet the whole top of your head would explode!"

And Dave was glad he'd said it, even if it wasn't nice, and even though it ended his experiment. Because after he said it, Lynsey stopped talking.

But the quiet only lasted about three seconds.

Lynsey said, "Is your *cough* all better? Because I thought I just heard a whiny little voice." She and her friends stared at Dave. "Did you say something?"

"Yeah, I did," he said. "I *said*, I bet if you had to shut up for five minutes, the top of your head would explode. Like a volcano. From all the hot gas that usually comes out of your mouth. When you talk

and talk and talk and never stop talking. Yeah. That's what I said. To you."

Lynsey tilted her head and looked at Dave, sort of the way a bird looks at a bug it's about to eat.

"Oh, like there's something *wrong* with talking? You never have any trouble with *yourself* blabbing and blabbing every day. We've all *heard* you." And the other girls nodded and made faces.

"Well," Dave said, "talking's okay, when there's stuff worth saying."

Lynsey said, "*Ohhh*—so *boys* can say things like, 'Hey, did you hear this guy got traded to that team, and that guy got traded to this team, and, hey, he hit real good last year, and, ooh yeah, he can really catch!' Boys can talk and talk like that, but girls can't talk about clothes sometimes? Is *that* it?"

Dave said, "No . . . but I don't talk the way you talk, like, for a million minutes in a row without stopping. And . . . and . . ."

Dave was hunting for something strong to say, a real punch line, something that would shut Lynsey up and end this conversation. So he said, ". . . and anyway, boys *never* talk as much as girls do, ever!"

Please take a careful look at that last thing Dave just said.

Because with this particular group of fifth

graders, *that* was a dangerous thing to say.

And now is a good time to tell a little more about the fifth-grade boys and the fifth-grade girls at Laketon Elementary School—to explain why it was a bad idea for Dave to say what he just said.

Because Dave should have kept his mouth shut.

He really should have.

CHAPTER 4

COOTIES

When little Dave Packer and all the other kids his age first showed up to begin kindergarten together, it was sort of like they were new recruits joining the army.

And kindergarten was sort of like basic training camp, except the teachers were a lot nicer than army drill instructors.

After nine long months together in kindergarten, Dave and the other new recruits were allowed to quit the army—but only for the summer. Because in September they all had to re-enlist for first grade.

And after first grade, they marched through second grade together, then third, and so on, right through the grades. Together. A few kids moved away, and a couple of new kids arrived, but Dave and those original kindergarten recruits stayed together, year after year. And they began to grow up. Together.

At most elementary schools, by the time a group gets to fifth grade, the boys have stopped thinking that all the girls have cooties, and the girls have stopped thinking that all the boys have cooties. And that's the way it should be—to outgrow that stuff.

For some groups, it's easy. The kids grow up a little bit, and they all learn that everyone's a real person, and some of those persons are boys and some are girls, and suddenly everyone gets along just fine, person to person. No more cooties.

However, some groups of kids cling to those cooties a little too long. The boys avoid the girls, and the girls avoid the boys, and everyone keeps seeing cooties everywhere. And, sadly, that's the way it was with most of the fifth-grade kids at Laketon Elementary School.

Of course, the fifth graders didn't actually use the word "cooties" anymore—that would have sounded like baby talk. They used words like "dumb" or "gross" or "immature" or "annoying." But a cootie by any other name is still a cootie.

And even worse, Dave and Lynsey were the king and queen of the fifth-grade cootie-clingers. Dave had zero tolerance for girls, and Lynsey had less-than-zero tolerance for boys.

And *that's* why Dave should have kept his mouth shut.

Now it's time to get back to the action in the lunchroom, because when Lynsey heard Dave say "boys never talk as much as girls do," she felt like all girls everywhere had been insulted, slapped in the face by a dumb, gross, immature, annoying boy. And she hadn't forgotten what Dave had already said, about the top of her head blowing off. Because of hot gas.

Lynsey wasn't the kind of person who forgives and forgets an insult. She was the kind of person who remembers. And then gets even.

CHAPTER 5

THE CONTEST

Lynsey narrowed her eyes and hissed, "You take that back!"

Dave shrugged. "Take what back? That girls are big blabberheads all the time? No way—because they *are*! Everybody knows that."

It's a shame to have to report this, but Dave actually believed what he was saying. And in his ignorant but creative young mind, an idea sparked to life.

Before Lynsey or any of her friends could say something back, Dave said, "And there's a way to *prove* that girls talk way more than boys. Unless you're afraid of some competition, you and your noisy friends."

"Afraid?" Lynsey said, looking around at the girls. "We're not afraid of anything—except catching whatever made *you* so stupid."

The girls giggled, but Dave ignored the insult, completely caught up by his new idea. He waved his hands to quiet them down. "Okay, here's the deal: a whole day of no talking at school. Not in class, not in the halls, not on the playground, nowhere. No talking at all. And it's a contest—boys against girls. Whichever side talks less, wins."

Lynsey made a face. "No talking? At school? That's impossible."

Dave had an advantage here. He had just spent almost four hours without saying a word. At school. So he had some experience, and he felt like he knew what he was talking about.

He grinned and said, "Maybe it's impossible for a *girl* to be quiet. But I bet the boys can do it. Or at least, we can do it better than the girls."

Lynsey said, "But, like, what if a teacher looked right at you and asked a question, then what?"

Dave grinned and said, "You could always . . . cough."

Lynsey's mouth dropped open, and then she glared at him. "You did that coughing in social studies *on purpose*? You are *so* immature!"

Dave shrugged. "It was sort of a test. And it worked. But if every kid in fifth grade coughed every time a teacher asked a question? *That* would *not* work."

Lynsey sniffed. "Well, *I* say that this whole idea is . . . childish. Silly and childish."

"It's okay if you don't want to," Dave said. "It was just an idea. I mean, I can see why you'd be afraid, since you're a girl and all. And since you *have* to talk every other second. No problem. Sorry I interrupted you. Just keep talking to your friends there. You were talking about something important, weren't you? That special sweater, right? Go ahead, talk. You girls go on and talk and talk and talk all you want to."

Lynsey pressed her lips together and glared at Dave, her eyes narrowed to slits. "You are the most annoying little—" She stopped mid-insult and folded her arms. "All right," she said. "Let's work out the rules. Right now. If a teacher talks to you, what then?"

"You answer," Dave said.

"How many words can you use?" she asked.

Dave smiled. "Let's make it . . . ten words—in case you and your friends need to tell a teacher about some new clothes you got."

"Stop trying to be funny. Because you're *not*," Lynsey said. "Make the limit four words. If you answer with more than four words in a row, the extras count."

Dave shook his head. "Four's still too easy. Let's make it a three-word limit. And every illegal word is one point—*against* your team."

"Duh," said Lynsey. "Like I needed you to explain that!"

"So it's a three-word limit?" Dave said.

"Three," said Lynsey, "and you can answer teachers, or the principal . . ."

". . . or any grown-up at school," said Dave. "Like the custodian."

"Or the nurse," added Lynsey. Because she wasn't about to let Dave Packer have the last word about anything.

"What about contractions?" she asked.

"What about 'em?" Dave said.

"Does a contraction count as one word or two?"

Dave didn't let it show in his face, but he was impressed by Lynsey's question—that she was able to think so far ahead and figure out that words like "won't" or "isn't" could cause a scorekeeping problem. And right away, Dave was just as impressed with himself, because he understood how to answer her question with a question of his own.

He said, "If you go find a dictionary, can you look up the word 'won't'?"

Lynsey nodded. "Of course you can."

"Then it's a word—one word," said Dave. "Any other questions?"

And now it was Lynsey's turn to hide her

thoughts, because she was impressed with Dave's answer. He was still *very* annoying, but his answer seemed right, plus he'd explained his reasoning clearly. But she didn't get carried away with good feelings about Dave. He was still a miserable, unpleasant boy who was forcing her to get involved in a pointless contest.

It's also a shame to have to report this, but Lynsey was just as proud and stubborn as Dave. And since he had pushed her into this fight, she felt it was her duty to push back—and she saw the perfect way to do it.

She turned away and whispered something to the girls at her lunch table, and when they all nodded their heads, she turned back to Dave. She gestured toward her friends and said, "*We* want to make this contest harder. How about this: no talking at home, either. Or on the school bus, or anywhere else. No talking at all—except for what we already decided. Not even to parents. And let's make the contest last for *two* days instead of one—two twenty-four-hour days in a row. Unless you think that's too *hard*."

Dave shrugged. "Fine, no problem. Except . . . how do we keep track of all the mess-ups when you and your friends start gabbing at home?"

"You mean, when the *boys* cheat?" said Lynsey.

"Simple. We'll have to use the honor system when we're not at school. It's the only way. We all keep track of our own mistakes. And report them. *Honestly*. Except I don't know if the *boys* can be trusted. Have any boys even *heard* of the honor system? I *know* you can trust the girls."

"Don't worry about us," Dave said.

Lynsey tossed her head. "So when does the contest start? The girls can be ready by tomorrow. At lunchtime. Unless that's too soon for the boys. Do you need more time to get organized? Like a week? Or *two* weeks?"

"Very funny," said Dave. "We'll start Tuesday, tomorrow. At the beginning of lunch. And it's not over until Thursday . . . how about at twelve fifteen? That'll be the middle of lunch period." Lynsey nodded, and Dave went on. "I'll be the official scorekeeper for our side, and you keep track for the girls. And no cheating. Okay?"

Lynsey nodded again. "Agreed." She held out her hand.

Dave looked at it like it was covered with slime. "What?" he said.

Lynsey wrinkled her nose. "It's *revolting*, but we have to shake on it—so *you* won't try to back out."

Dave shook, and then made a show of wiping his

hand on his pants, which got a big laugh from the five or six other boys who had witnessed the ceremony.

And as Dave turned and went into a huddle with the guys at his lunch table, Lynsey did the same with the girls at her table.

The contest was on.

CHAPTER 6

TEAMWORK

The boys Dave ate lunch with were his best friends. He looked around at them and grinned after he'd explained the rules. "Cool contest, huh?"

Todd shook his head. "I'm not doing this—it's dumb. Who wants to not talk? Besides, it's impossible, like she said."

"You think girls *can* stop talking, but boys *can't*?" Dave asked. "So you're just giving up without a fight? Is that it?"

Todd said, "Well, no . . . but it's still a stupid idea."

"So what?" said Dave. "It's a *contest*, and the boys are gonna win it, okay? So listen. First, we've got to tell every guy. Everybody *has* to be with us on this. Tim Flanagan was absent in homeroom this morning. I'll call him, in case he's coming back tomorrow. And you all have to do that too, figure out who else isn't

136

here. And if you don't have a number, call me at home tonight, 'cause my mom has a school directory. And every fifth-grade boy who's here at school has to be told. Today. Okay?"

Jason said, "But really, not talking? For two days? Like . . . how?"

Dave pulled an index card from his pocket. On the back of his India report he wrote the word "Easy." He held it up, showing it to all the boys.

Then he said, "Did I just talk?"

"No," said Jason.

Dave said, "Keep watching."

He shook his head.

Then he nodded at them.

Then he smiled.

Then he frowned and showed his teeth and growled like a dog.

"I didn't talk, right? But you *got* what I said. Not talking just means . . . not talking. It'll probably be fun—but even if it's not, it's a *contest*. Against the girls. And we're gonna win it, right? And tell all the guys to practice short sentences. Three words or less."

Jim said, "You bug me!"

Jason said, "Your breath smells!"

Richard said, "Look, it's Batman!—hey, is Batman one word or two?"

And the sentences kept coming, each boy trying to be the goofiest.

"Guys," Dave said. "Guys, c'mon. We've only got fourteen minutes before next period. *All* the fifth-grade boys are right here at lunch—it's the perfect chance to tell everyone. And I hate to tell you, but the girls are already ahead of us."

The boys hushed, and looked around.

Lynsey, Anna, Emily, Taron—all the friends who'd been sitting at the next table were fanning out through the cafeteria, talking to every girl in sight. And Hannah and Karin were heading for the door to the playground.

Dave said, "Everybody know what you have to say to our team?"

The boys looked back at him and nodded, each face deadly serious now.

"All right, then," Dave said. "Let's do this."

CHAPTER 7

THE UNSHUSHABLES

Since Dave and Lynsey had been almost shout-ing at each other in the middle of the cafeteria, you might think that a lot of the other fifth graders in the room would have tuned in and paid attention to the commotion. You might think that a lot of the kids in the lunchroom already knew about the contest.

But if you thought that, you'd be wrong.

And you'd be wrong because you don't understand just how *loud*, how incredibly *noisy* it was in the cafeteria during fifth-grade lunch. And not just on this one day. It was noisy during fifth-grade lunch *every* day.

And it wasn't noisy only at lunch. *Anywhere* a bunch of these fifth graders got together, the talking got out of hand.

That's why it's time to tell a little more about

this particular set of fifth-grade kids.

Because there's more to tell. There's *always* more.

A school system really is a little like the army—remember? About how kindergarten is sort of like basic training camp?

Because kindergarten was where Dave and the other new recruits first learned the rules. They learned when to sit and when to stand, when to talk and when to hush, when to walk and when to run, when to eat, and nap, and play, and sing, and draw, and everything else.

Because every system needs rules—no rules, no system.

Most of the rules made perfect sense to Dave and the new recruits, especially rules like this: no fighting, no bullying, no shoving, no spitting, no biting, no stealing, no vandalism, no cutting in line, no snowball throwing, and so on.

For most kids, the really serious rules like that weren't hard at all. Those were the easy ones.

The toughest rules were ones like, "No running in the halls."

Hard.

"No disorderly behavior on the buses."

Also hard.

"No candy or chewing gum."

Very hard.

But nowhere in the forty-four-page Laketon Elementary School Handbook did it actually say, "No whispering, chatting, talking, calling out, yelling, or shouting in classrooms, in the hallways, in the auditorium, or in the lunchroom."

True, there *was* a rule about paying attention in class. And there *was* a rule about being respectful. And there *was* a rule about being courteous at all times.

And Dave and his classmates obeyed those rules— or at least, they *thought* they did. It's just that they all seemed to think they could talk *and* be courteous— at the same time. And they all seemed to think they could talk *and* pay attention—at the same time.

Because none of these kids really meant to be disrespectful or disobedient or discourteous. But none of them wanted to stop talking. Ever.

In fact, this group of kids had been given a nick-name by the teachers at Laketon Elementary School, and the name had stuck with them ever since they had all been in first grade together. They were "The Unshushables."

If Laketon Elementary School had *really* been like the army, then sometime—probably during second grade—Dave and Lynsey and all the other recruits would have been lined up out on the playground on a cold, rainy morning, and a gruff man with short hair and shiny shoes would have walked up and down in front of them, shouting right into their faces. And he would have shouted something like this:

"YOU DRIVE ME *CRAZY*! You call yourselves *STUDENTS*? You are a MISERABLE *MOB*! You are LOUD, UNdisciplined, and I WILL not tolerate your NOISE! When you walk in MY hallways, you do not SHOUT! You do not WAVE and YELL and HOOT when you see your friends. At an assembly in MY school, you do NOT whisper and giggle and point and wave and laugh at your own silly jokes! And when you come to MY lunchroom, it is NOT a free-for-all festival of flap-jawed jibber-jabber! Lunch is a time to SIT and be QUIET and EAT. I am going to TEACH you little motormouth MONSTERS proper school MANNERS if it is THE LAST

THING I DO! DO I MAKE MYSELF
CLEAR?"
  "YES, SIR!"
"QUIETER!"
"Yes, sir!"

But, of course, Laketon Elementary School wasn't
the army.

However, with Mrs. Abigail Hiatt in charge,
sometimes it felt that way. She was a tall woman with
a long face, curly gray hair, and bright blue eyes, and
she had been the principal at Laketon Elementary
School for the past thirteen years.

She gave careful orders, set precise goals, and she
demanded results from her teachers, from her office
staff, from her custodians, from her cafeteria workers,
and from her students and their parents, too. Her
school never went over its budget, never missed its
academic targets, and the place never felt loose or
sloppy or disorderly.

Under Mrs. Hiatt's watchful eye, group after
group of children had wandered into Laketon
Elementary School as aimless little kindergartners
and marched out six years later as perfectly disci-
plined young students. Under Mrs. Hiatt's leadership, the place ran like clockwork.

And then the Unshushables came along. In all her years as principal she had never known a group of kids like this.

And for the past five years, Mrs. Hiatt had been trying to make these kids obey the simplest school rule of all: no talking—except when it's allowed.

Year after year, memos had been sent home to the parents of Dave and his classmates about too much shouting on the school buses.

Year after year, Dave's grade had been told how to behave before every assembly.

Year after year, all their teachers had stood out in the hallways to try to keep the noise down before and after school, and especially at lunchtime.

This group had even been given a separate lunch period for the past three years in a row: third-grade lunch, fourth-grade lunch, and this year, fifth-grade lunch. Mrs. Hiatt had made that decision. She didn't want the noisy behavior of this group to infect the other children at her school. Because year after year, the Unshushables lived up to their nickname.

To be honest, a few of this year's fifth-grade teachers had already given up. They didn't have any real hope of changing these kids. They were just trying to cope. Because it was already November, so in six short months the Unshushables would be gone forever, moved along to the junior high, and next year Laketon Elementary School would be quieter. *Much* quieter.

But Mrs. Hiatt had not given up, not by a long shot. She still had over half a year with these kids, and she intended to use that time.

Every day the principal stalked the fifth-grade hall. "*You there*—stop shouting!"

At every assembly, she glared. "And I don't want to hear even a *whisper* from our fifth graders, is that clear?"

At every fifth-grade lunch, she walked around the cafeteria with a big red plastic bullhorn, and when the noise became unbearable, she pulled the trigger and bellowed, "STUDENTS! YOU ARE TALKING TOO LOUD!"

Mrs. Hiatt felt sure that this constant reminding *had* to be having an effect on these kids . . . how could it not? After all, these were good kids . . . right? They *had* to be making progress . . . didn't they?

She knew she was being very stern with them, but it was for their own good. And Mrs. Hiatt felt sure that sooner or later, these kids would grow up a little—and quiet down a lot.

· · ·

And now it's time to tell what happened in the middle of the second Tuesday in November during Dave Packer's final year at Laketon Elementary School.

It was two minutes before fifth-grade lunch, and the principal was ready, just like always. Mrs. Hiatt had checked to be sure that the other teacher who had fifth-grade lunch duty wasn't out sick or at a meeting. Because it wasn't good to try to manage fifth-grade lunch all by yourself.

And, just like always, she had ordered Mr. Lipton, the custodian, to stay in the cafeteria today until 12:40. Because with this group, the more grown-ups around, the better.

And Mrs. Hiatt had double-checked the batteries in her red plastic bullhorn. Because it wasn't good to have a dead bullhorn during fifth-grade lunch.

Then the bell rang, and as classroom doors along the fifth-grade hall flew open, Mrs. Hiatt could hear them coming, all of them, already calling to each other as locker doors clanged open and banged shut, already talking a mile a minute, already laughing and whooping and shouting, streaming down the hall-way toward the cafeteria, an unshushable wave of energy and excitement and noise . . . *so much noise!*

Mrs. Hiatt took her position at the center of the cafeteria and braced herself. She was ready for today's lunchroom battle, ready to change chaos into order, ready for anything these kids could dish out.

But nothing could have prepared her for what happened next.

CHAPTER 8

SCIENCE FICTION

It was four minutes into the fifth-grade lunch period, and Mrs. Hiatt was pretty sure that any second now, her alarm clock was going to start making that awful sound—**BRRAP! BRRAP! BRRAP! BRRAP!**

Because the principal was almost certain that she was still at home in her own comfy bed, dreaming away. She *had* to be dreaming. But no, she looked at her watch and it showed the same time as the large clock above the stage in the school cafeteria—12:04.

On any other day Mrs. Hiatt would have already used her bullhorn at least once, because when half the fifth graders were standing in the food line, and the other half were in the milk line or rushing toward their seats, there was always a terrific burst of yelling and calling out and wild chatter—sort of like feeding time at the zoo.

Not today.

There was no talking at all. Not one word. Over one hundred twenty-five children milling around the lunchroom, and not a peep from any of them.

Today the principal could hear the clattering of the worn-out motor in the milk cooler. And she could hear the kitchen workers talking softly to each other. And she could hear the children's feet on the tile floor, shuffling along through the lines.

The quiet almost frightened her. Mrs. Hiatt felt like she was in a scene from a creepy science fiction movie.

She actually liked a good scary movie now and then, but she did *not* like the ideas in her mind at this moment. Because it seemed like aliens had possessed these fifth graders and zapped their brains. Or maybe some strange creature had nipped off all their tongues—nothing left but little stubs that couldn't make a sound.

The principal shivered. Then she noticed a girl staring at her. Mrs. Hiatt realized she must have had a strange look on her face.

As the girl sat down with her lunch tray, Mrs. Hiatt forced herself to smile, and said, "Hi there, Sheila. How are you today?" Her voice almost echoed in the quiet lunchroom.

Every boy in the milk line turned and stared at

Sheila. The girls turned and looked too.

Sheila gulped, gave the principal a nervous smile, and, speaking softly and slowly, she said, "Fine, thank you."

Mrs. Hiatt turned toward the milk line, and all the kids looked away. Silently.

And again, the principal felt like she was in the middle of a science fiction movie.

It suddenly seemed silly to be standing there in a silent room with her huge red plastic bullhorn. So Mrs. Hiatt walked over to the playground door, where Mrs. Escobar was standing. She tried to look as casual as possible, tried to act like it was perfectly normal for the lunchroom to be stone silent except for the clattering of plates and the squeaking of sneakers on the waxed floor.

The principal set the bullhorn on the floor by the wall and whispered to Mrs. Escobar, "What in the world is going on here?"

Mrs. Escobar whispered back, "I have no idea. But it's something weird, that's for sure."

Mrs. Hiatt did not like this feeling, this feeling that something strange, something new was happening. Because this new activity was happening at her school, and no one had asked for her permission. This new activity was unauthorized.

Mrs. Hiatt didn't simply *like* being in charge of her own school. She felt like she *needed* to be in charge.

And that's why she felt like she had to say something, do something, to break the spell. So she stepped away from the wall and in a loud voice she said, "Good afternoon, fifth graders. Are you enjoying your lunchtime today?"

All the kids looked at each other. The whole room seemed to take a deep breath, and then almost everyone said, "Yes, Mrs. Hiatt."

And then silence again.

After an awkward few seconds, the principal said, "It's so *quiet* in here today. I'm very . . . impressed. With your good behavior."

Some kids smiled, some nodded. But no one said a word.

Mrs. Hiatt said, "Is there some special reason why no one's talking today?"

The whole room went still. Even the chewing stopped.

No hands went up, and no one answered her question.

But Mrs. Hiatt was a keen observer, and in that sudden stillness she noticed something. Right after she asked her question, it seemed like almost every boy looked at Dave Packer, who was standing beside the milk cooler. And it seemed like almost every girl took a quick look at Lynsey Burgess, who was just sitting down at a table.

And the principal thought, *That's odd*.

But the whole situation was odd. Very odd. And now it seemed like the room was stuck in a complete calm, as if all the kids had even stopped breathing.

Everyone was waiting to see what she was going to do next.

After a few more seconds of suspense, Mrs. Hiatt cleared her throat and said, "Well, students, please enjoy the rest of your lunchtime."

And the cafeteria came back to life. Silently.

CHAPTER 9

THE RIGHT WORD

As Dave sat down at a lunch table with his friends, he couldn't get the grin off his face. He was having so much fun he could hardly chew his first bite of grilled cheese. And he didn't like chewing right now because chewing made noise, and when he munched he couldn't hear the silence.

The *silence*—Dave thought it was amazing.

And watching Mrs. Hiatt try to figure out what was going on? That was amazing too. It was like they had trapped her in a force field. And she couldn't get out of it, because the silence filled the cafeteria.

Dave looked around, and he saw the same amazement on the faces of some other kids. They were all thinking about the same thing. Together.

Then suddenly: "Hey, give it back!"

There was a gasp as every boy and girl in the

room sucked in a breath, and all heads turned to see where those words had come from.

And there at the ice cream freezer, Ed Kesey had one hand over his mouth while his other hand reached for a cherry Popsicle that Bryan DelGreco had grabbed.

Dave swung around and looked at Lynsey.

Lynsey knew a lot of kids were watching her, but she pretended not to notice. She slowly reached into her back pocket, slowly pulled out a pen and a small red notebook, slowly opened the cover, and slowly made four little marks on the first page.

And as she flipped the notebook shut, Lynsey looked right at Dave and gave him a big smile.

Just like that, and the girls were ahead by four points.

But Dave wasn't worried. The contest had barely begun. There were two whole days to go.

Dave was absolutely sure that the next forty-eight hours were going to be very . . . *interesting.* And he thought, *Is that the right word? How about . . . fascinating? No, more like . . . exciting. Yeah—exciting!*

Then Dave happened to glance at Mrs. Hiatt. And he could tell from the look on the principal's face that she had been watching everything—the way Ed had shouted those words and then covered his mouth, the way all the other kids had reacted, the way Lynsey had marked her notebook.

And at that exact moment the principal turned and locked eyes with Dave. She stared right at him, with her eyebrows all bunched up in a puzzled knot.

Dave quickly looked down at his lunch tray, and as he did, a new word popped into his mind. And he was pretty sure this one was also going to be a good word to describe the next few days: *dangerous.*

CHAPTER 10

RECESS

Mrs. Marlow was the fifth-grade science teacher, and it was her day for outdoor recess duty. As she was gulping down a quick lunch in the teachers' room, Mr. Lipton, the custodian, stuck his head in the door and said, "Anybody want to see a miracle? Go check out the cafeteria. The fifth graders aren't talking today—not even whispering. It's like a funeral in there."

But Mrs. Marlow didn't have a moment to spare. She finished her lunch, grabbed her coat, and hurried outside to the playground through the gym.

Even without the heads-up from the custodian, it wouldn't have taken her long to figure out that something was different at outside recess today. Every teacher knows the sound of a normal, happy playground at lunchtime—kids talking and yelling and chasing, and all the arguments about who's it and who's out and who ran faster.

Not today. Mrs. Marlow could tell that a whole layer of spoken sound was missing. Gone. Absent.

Except . . . not completely. Because the kids did make some slipups during their first wordless recess.

Allie Bedford got caught whispering to Lena Henderson by the swing set, and when a group of boys stood and shook their fingers at her, she held up eight fingers to show how many illegal words she had said.

Christina Farley didn't have to confess, because half the kids on the playground heard exactly what she said, loud and clear. She stomped her feet, stuck out her tongue at Rachel Morgan, and then shouted, "You're a terrible friend, and you lie, and you're self-ish, and I don't care how many words this is! And you're *mean,* too!"

Which was twenty-three words.

Christina's goof, plus the eight words Allie whispered, meant that Dave got to record thirty-one points against the girls on his official score sheet, which wasn't as fancy as Lynsey's red notebook—just a couple of folded index cards stuffed in his pocket.

But the boys weren't perfect either.

Scott Vickers booted a kickball down the third-base line, and when two boys made the "foul ball" motion, he yelled, "Foul? Are you *crazy*? No *way*! That ball was fair!" And Scott would have kept on yelling, but Bill Harkness tackled him and clamped a hand over his mouth—which Scott bit, but not hard enough to make Bill yell any words.

That incident cost the boys ten points.

And then there was the first case of trickery. Katie Edison snuck up behind Jeremy Stephens, who was standing by the sliding board, tapped him on the shoulder, and when he turned his head, she gave him a big, noisy kiss on the cheek.

Jeremy howled and wiped his face and flew into a fit of cootie-itis. "Eeew, *YUCK!* Why did you *do* that? That was so *gross*! *YUCK!* Help me get this stuff off my face!"

Which was twenty more points for the girls. Plus Katie actually enjoyed her sneak attack—she'd had a top secret crush on Jeremy for two months.

Even though there were only a few word blasts, it certainly wasn't quiet out there, and it got noisier and noisier as the end of recess got closer. That's because everyone began to realize that this was not a contest to see who could be silent. It was just about not talking. Sounds were allowed—as long as they weren't words.

Dave was near the door of the gym and began whistling. He was instantly joined by four other boys. They whistled every song they could think of—"Row, Row, Row Your Boat"; "Now I Know My ABCs"; "London Bridge Is Falling Down"; Barney's "Marching Song"; the *Star Wars* theme song; "Old MacDonald Had a Farm"; "I've Been Working on the Railroad"; "Rubber Ducky"—on and on. The whistling was mostly off-key, but it was a grand performance anyway, with lots of clapping and hooting between tunes.

Somewhere near the middle of the whistling concert, six or seven girls began screaming. These were not the kind of screams that make grown-ups come running. They were just an ugly assortment of squeals and yelps and shrieks that everyone else found very annoying. Spaced out around the edge of the playground, the girls bounced their high-pitched sounds around like a beach ball at a baseball stadium: "EeeeOww!" "OooWhee!" "WooHoooh!" "Yeeyeeyeeyeee!" They made lots of noise, but they weren't talking.

Some other girls were jumping double Dutch, and since they couldn't chant the rhymes, the kids who weren't jumping or turning the ropes clapped out the rhythm of the words with their hands.

The quietest activity involved four girls who had a printed folder that showed how to use American Sign Language. They sat in a circle on the ground and practiced their hand signals.

And to round out the soundscape, Bradley Lang and Tyler Rennert were cruising around the playground bothering as many girls as possible by making all sorts of mouth sounds—clicks, pops, roars, quacks, barks, burps, and especially those loud bathroom noises created by putting the palms of both hands over the mouth, puffing up the cheeks, and blooping out a blast of air.

Mrs. Marlow could see there was plenty of activity, but those high-pitched playground voices, all that buzz and chatter and calling out, all that was definitely missing. There was no mistaking it: These kids were not talking, which would have been unusual for any bunch of students. For *this* group of kids, the custodian had called it right: It was practically a miracle.

But why? There had to be a reason they were all acting this way. And as a science-minded person, Mrs. Marlow was curious.

So, as she stood there thinking, Mrs. Marlow

began to adjust her afternoon lesson plan. Because in about ten minutes, twenty-six of these fifth graders would be sitting in her room, ready for science class.

And there was nothing Mrs. Marlow liked better than a good experiment.

CHAPTER 11

QUESTIONS
AND ANSWERS

In all her years of teaching—seventeen in total—Mrs. Marlow had never walked into a quieter classroom full of students. It was a new experience for her.

It was also new for the kids.

Dave watched Mrs. Marlow go to the front of the room and pick up her attendance book. The teacher looked at the list of names in the book, looked up and down the rows of the class, looked at the book again, and said, "I thought maybe I was in the wrong room. Pretty quiet in here today. Can someone tell me why?"

No hands went up.

But Mrs. Marlow was watching for anything that might give her a clue about this unusual behavior.

And after her question, she saw a few sly glances between kids, and she noticed some of them trying to hide a smile. She knew what those looks and smiles meant: These kids were keeping a secret.

Time for her first experiment.

Looking over the class, Mrs. Marlow settled her eyes on Seth Townsend, smiled, and said, "So, Seth, did you do your science homework last night?"

With no hesitation, Seth smiled back and said, "Yes, I did."

Mrs. Marlow looked at Amy Gilson and said, "How about you, Amy?"

She nodded and said, "It was hard."

"Really? What did you think was hard about it?" she asked.

Amy scrunched up her face and then said, "Too much math."

Her answer got a lot of nods and a few laughs from the other kids, but then it went completely quiet again.

Mrs. Marlow couldn't get over how beautifully these children were behaving. Just yesterday, she had asked one student a question, and about fifteen others had blurted out answers, and then the whole class began arguing, and that had started a huge free-for-all that didn't end until she banged on her desk with a book. It was always like that with this class, and with the other fifth-grade classes too.

But not today. No one talked at all . . . *unless* she asked a question.

Which gave Mrs. Marlow an idea.

"Please get out your homework sheets."

There was a lot of rustling and bustling as the students obeyed.

"Now," she said. "Ellen, look at problem number one. How did you decide if the given quantities were reasonable?"

Ellen riffled through her papers, and the look on her face surprised Mrs. Marlow: Ellen looked scared.

It was one of the standard questions about science problems, a question the whole class was used to. But the girl seemed completely confused. Mrs. Marlow could see that she'd done the assignment. Plus, Ellen was one of the best science students. What was she so scared about?

After a few moments of what looked like absolute panic, Ellen calmed down. Then, very slowly, she said, "The numbers . . . worked."

Mrs. Marlow waited for the rest of her explanation. It didn't come.

"Right," she said, "and . . ."

"I . . . made estimates," Ellen said.

Again, her words came slowly. And then there was another long pause.

"And . . . ," the teacher urged.

"I used . . . math."

Mrs. Marlow nodded. "Of course you used math. But I want to hear about your *process*, your *thinking*."

Ellen said, "I did . . . comparing."

Frustrated, Mrs. Marlow turned to the other side of the room. "Dave, tell us the answer you got for problem one. And explain your *process*."

Dave didn't look scared, but he also took a long time to respond—too long for Mrs. Marlow. She said, "I'd like your answer *today*, Mr. Packer."

Slowly, Dave said, "Four hundred forty."

" 'Four hundred forty' what?" prompted Mrs. Marlow.

"Barrels of oil," said Dave. Slowly.

"Per . . . ," said Mrs. Marlow.

Dave said, "Per . . . day."

"Wrong," said Mrs. Marlow. "Look at your work and tell me what you forgot." She was losing her patience.

Dave frowned and squinted at his paper. He nodded and then slowly said, "Um . . . the first day."

A ripple of giggles swept through the room—girl giggles.

Mrs. Marlow snapped, "Since when did wrong answers become funny?"

The science teacher thought, *Are they all pretending to be stupid today? Is that it?*

Whatever was going on, she didn't like it. It was disruptive. It was slowing down her class. It was annoying.

And suddenly Mrs. Marlow was in no mood for games. She was *not* going to play along. If these kids wanted quiet, then that's what they were going to get.

She glared around the room. "Pass in your papers."

Everyone obeyed without a word.

"Open to chapter four and read. The homework is on the board."

The next thirty-four minutes in the science room passed in complete silence, except for the rustle of paper and an occasional cough or sniffle.

And sitting at her desk, Mrs. Marlow had to admit that she enjoyed the quiet, enjoyed not having to fight the battle of the mouth every second with these kids. The Unshushables were completely shushed, all right—very weird.

But the science teacher wasn't any closer to figuring out *why* the kids were acting this way.

Dave felt something hit his arm and then drop onto his leg. It was a note.

He glanced at Mrs. Marlow. All clear. So he slowly reached down, picked up the note, and unfolded it.

> You said, "Um, the first day."
> Um counts as a word.
> So you said four, and you cost the boys one whole point—loser!
>   Ha-ha!
>   Lynsey

Dave knew Lynsey was sitting two seats back on his left. And he knew she was waiting for him to turn around so she could give him a sickly-sweet little smile.

So he didn't turn around. But he felt the tops of his ears getting pink. And he began thinking of a million things he wished he could say to her—all sorts of clever insults, like, *If brains were money, you'd be broke,* or *Wow—you can count to four!* or *I had a pet turtle that* . . .

"Mr. Packer—bring it here."

Dave snapped to attention and looked up to see Mrs. Marlow staring at him, holding out her hand.

Putting on his best innocent face, Dave said, "What?"

"The note. Here."

As Dave walked up and dropped the note into Mrs. Marlow's hand, the bell rang.

Mrs. Marlow tucked the paper into her pocket and then stood up quickly. Because when the bell rang, she had to hurry out her door and try to maintain law and order in the hallway between classes.

But, of course, there was no need for the corridor police, not today. Mrs. Marlow watched all the fifth graders move from room to room, smiling, waving, making faces, nodding at each other. There were a few laughs and whistles, and she heard Tyler Rennert make a loud snort in the general direction of some girls, but there was no talking.

She looked across the hall and caught Mrs. Escobar's eye, and they both smiled and then shrugged at each other. And since there wasn't any patrol work to do, Mrs. Marlow reached into her pocket and pulled out the captured note. And she read it.

For a logical person like Mrs. Marlow, Lynsey's note to Dave was like the Rosetta stone, a key that helped her begin to understand what she had seen and heard on the playground and then in her classroom.

So . . . this whole thing was something about counting words. More than three words resulted in a penalty—which explained all those short answers from Ellen and Dave. And it was the boys against the girls—nothing new about that, not with this group. And they were all trying to keep quiet.

Mrs. Marlow remembered the "jinx" game from her own school years, when two people said the same word at the same time and then had to keep quiet. Maybe it was like that.

Except this wasn't two people. It was more than a hundred and twenty-five of the most talkative children on planet Earth.

As chunks of the puzzle began to fall into place, Mrs. Marlow immediately thought, *The others are going to love this!*

She meant the other teachers.

But then her scientific curiosity kicked in, and she thought, *Why spoil the kids' experiment? And I should really let the other teachers figure things out on their own. And, of course, my preliminary findings could be wrong. I should certainly gather more data before I present my theory to the scholarly community.*

And as Mrs. Marlow chuckled at her private joke, she said to herself, *Kids!*

CHAPTER 12

GUESSING GAMES

Tuesday afternoon in the fifth-grade hall was a challenge for everyone.

Mrs. Akers walked into the music room, sat at her piano, smiled, and said, "My, you are all behaving so *well* this afternoon—wonderful! Now, please open your songbooks to 'This Land Is Your Land.'"

As she played the introduction on the piano, she said, "Backs straight, big smiles, deep breaths, and . . ."

No one sang.

The piano stopped mid-measure, and Mrs. Akers frowned at the class. "Now, I *know* you can all do better than that."

She began the introduction again, counting in the beats. "One, and two, and three, 'This land is your land, this land . . .'"

Mrs. Akers stopped. She was singing a solo, and

her high, quivering voice made the kids giggle.

She frowned again. "All right, students. This is *not* funny. And it's not good. We have less than two weeks before our Thanksgiving program, and we have no time for this kind of silliness."

She pointed a bright pink fingernail around the room. "Brian, Tommy, Anna, every one of you! I want to hear you *sing!*"

She banged out the introduction again, and the whole class sang, "This land is . . ." and then stopped.

The piano kept playing, and Mrs. Akers bellowed, "Sing!" And most of the kids jumped in on ". . . my land, from . . ." and then stopped.

After another shouted command, they sang ". . . the redwood forest . . . ," and that's how the whole song went, chopped up into three-word bits.

And when Mrs. Akers, her face bright red by this point, thumped on her piano and said, "What is *wrong* with all of you today?" the kids didn't say a word.

Like all teachers, Mrs. Akers understood the "divide and conquer" rule: When you need to get to the bottom of something, you don't ask the whole class; you ask *one* student. So she pointed at Lena in the front row and said, "Why aren't you singing?"

Lena hesitated, and then motioned at the kids all around the room and said, "Not talking today."

Mrs. Akers said, "What's that supposed to mean? Not talking?"

Lena nodded. "Only three words."

The music teacher was even more puzzled. She pointed at James and said, "Explain."

James had trouble expressing himself even under the best conditions. He gulped and took a deep breath. Then he said, "Not . . . words. Everyone."

A light dawned on Mrs. Akers's face. And, still talking to James, she said, "Oh—so, is it like that project kids do, when they take a vow of silence? To protest how there's still slavery in Africa? I read about that—is that it?"

James looked lost. He shook his head. "Hard . . . explain. Not."

But Mrs. Akers felt like she had answered the riddle, or maybe partly answered it. And whatever was happening, she decided to be a good sport.

Looking around the room, she said, "So, tell me—can you all hum? Is humming allowed?"

Everyone grinned and nodded like maniacs.

"How about clapping? Can you clap in rhythm?" More smiles and nods.

"All right, then, here we go again," and she ripped back into the piano. "One, and two, and three! Hmm hmm hmm hmmm hmmm . . ."

And twenty-four fifth graders clapped and hummed along as Mrs. Akers played all seven verses of "This Land Is Your Land." Then the whole class giggled and laughed and hummed and clapped their way through the other four songs on the Thanksgiving program.

And they all survived their first wordless music class.

The fifth-period gym class was less dramatic than music. News had gotten to most of the teachers that the fifth graders had gone quiet, which didn't bother the gym teacher at all. Tuesday was dodgeball day, so Mrs. Henley appointed the two captains, and then the captains picked their teams by pointing, and the first game got under way—all without a word.

Dodgeball, which can be pretty serious anyway, seemed especially grim without the talking and shouting. There were the usual grunts of effort and screams of terror, and when three or four kids with red dodgeballs would silently go hunting for one player on the other team, it was sort of like watching a pack of wolves go after a lone caribou: A motion of the leader's head, a movement toward the prey, and then, *Whack! Whack! WHOMP!*—dead meat.

From the gym teacher's point of view, dodgeball was all about improving reflexes and getting a good large-motor-skills workout, and to accomplish those goals without any of the taunting and teasing and name-calling? That was just fine by her.

Even so, Mrs. Henley watched all three games with great interest, and she saw how the kids communicated without words. And she noticed herself pointing and shaking her head and blowing her whistle instead of yelling. It was nice to give her voice a rest.

Mr. Burton taught fifth-grade reading and language arts. He was puzzled at the beginning of the class right after lunch, and like the music teacher and the science teacher, he asked questions and got three-word answers. But he kept at it, and after about five minutes, he figured out what was going on, at least part of it.

Unlike Mrs. Marlow, Mr. Burton had a lot of patience and a pretty good sense of humor. And he couldn't see any real problem with having these kids be this well-behaved. Anything that got the Unshushables quiet was fine by him. Plus, he decided they could all have some fun with this limit of three words in a row.

He picked a funny story from their reading textbook, a really short one, and he had the kids read it out loud, three words each and as fast as possible, with him calling out the name of the next narrator.

And when the story was finished, he said, "Okay, now I want *you* to make up a story." He picked up a meter stick and said, "When I point at you, say a three-word sentence. And listen carefully, so you can make the story move forward. Here we go."

The story started like this:

"A woman screamed."

"She was scared."

"It was dark."

"'Oh, no—snakes!'"

"One bit her."

"'Ow! My leg!'"

"She limped outside."

"Her neighbor came."

"'What's wrong?'"

"'Snakes are everywhere!'"

"'Are they poisonous?'"

"'Yes, and smelly!'"

"'Quick, my car!'"

"'You saved me!'"

"'Darn! Dead battery!'"

Round and round the room the story went.

The poor woman and her neighbor were eventually eaten by the huge orange lizards that came up out of the sewers and ripped the roof off the car. The lizards also ate all the snakes. But then some ugly

tulips in the garden grew razor-blade teeth and ate the lizards. And then the tulips burped giant burps, which created a tornado that made the Statue of Liberty fall over and crush a tugboat, which made a wave that washed all the way to the White House and got muddy water all over the president's polka-dotted underpants.

It was quite a tale.

The period ended, and as the students walked quietly out of the room, Mr. Burton got a lot of waves and smiles and thumbs-ups. And he waved and smiled back at the kids. No words were needed.

It had been a successful class—fun, creative, lively, and everyone had used their word skills in new ways. Mr. Burton felt great.

The next forty minutes was his planning period, and then came the last class of the day, period seven. He had some papers to grade, but Mr. Burton was too excited. Because what these kids were doing— well, it felt like a once-in-a-lifetime chance to mess around with words and language and communica-tion, to try something fresh, something special. After all, science teachers aren't the only people who like a good experiment.

So Mr. Burton sat at his desk, thinking and think-ing. Finally, with about two minutes before period seven, he got it—a great idea. Plus, he realized that this situation could be useful to him in a totally unexpected way.

And as the bell rang, Mr. Burton noticed that he was actually looking forward to his last class of the afternoon—another proof that this was *not* an ordinary day.

CHAPTER 13

LANGUAGE LAB

As his last class of the day came into Mr. Burton's room, he didn't speak, and of course, neither did the students.

The bell rang, and all the kids watched him as he put a stack of lined paper on the front desk of each row. Then he turned to the chalkboard and began to write.

Today there will be <u>writing only</u>. Nothing will be turned in, but everyone <u>must</u> write all period long, and everyone must communicate with at least four other people.
<u>You may not stop writing for more than fifteen seconds.</u>
As soon as you have paper, begin.

In less than one minute, every kid had paper. And in less than two minutes, the first notes were changing hands.

Todd wrote, "I still think this no talking thing is stupid," and he passed the paper to Kyle.

Kyle read the note and wrote, "I sorta like it. It's different. A challenge."

And then Todd wrote, "Challenge? What challenge? The teachers already know about it. Like Mr. Burton. He's just messing with us. Thinks it's great we're not talking. I LIKE TALKING!"

Kyle read, and he wrote back, "Too bad. Think how hard it is for all the blabby girls—we're gonna win this contest. Beat the girls! Beat the girls! Beat the girls! Get it? It's a silent cheer, like at a basketball game. Cool, huh?"

Todd wrote back, "Cool? Dude, it's lame. Here's my silent cheer—Kyle's a Dork! Kyle's a Dork! Kyle's a Dork!"

Kyle read the note, made a face at Todd, and then turned his back on him and started up a chat with Eric. No talking made it very simple to tune someone out.

A few seats away, Emily was having a hot argument with Taron. "I did not say you couldn't come over after school. I just said what's the point? If we can't talk. That's all."

Taron read the note, shook her head, and wrote, "I <u>know</u> you don't like me as much as you like Kelly. So stop pretending."

Emily rolled her eyes and wrote, "Don't be like that."

Taron shrugged and wrote, "Like what?"

Emily used block letters for emphasis. "ALL SNIFFY AND SNOOFY AND OUCHY—I <u>HATE</u> THAT."

"See?" Taron wrote. "<u>Hate</u>. That's what you said. You hate me."

Emily scribbled, "Don't be an idiot! I <u>don't</u> hate you. Come over after school. Really. We'll think of something to do. But we're gonna want to talk. I know we will. And we can't."

And Taron wrote back, "I'm NOT coming. <u>You</u> think I'm an <u>idiot</u>."

Emily read that, and then ripped the paper to pieces. And she reached across the aisle and patted Taron on the arm, and smiled her warmest smile, and then wrote on a fresh sheet of paper, "After school. My house, okay?"

Taron smiled back and nodded.

All around the room, kids were having to figure out the new rules for communicating. And for most of them, writing was a lot harder than talking. It was slower, like instant messaging—only less instant, and less fun because there was no computer to mess with. There was so much less give-and-take than there was with talking. The Unshushables weren't used to that. At all.

Dave had just finished a frustrating set of back-and-forth messages with Bill.

Bill couldn't understand how to keep from getting called offside during a soccer game. Dave had explained it three different ways. He had drawn pictures and diagrams and everything, and Bill still couldn't figure it out.

So Dave passed a note to Ed, because he was the best junior league player in town. "Bill doesn't get the offside rule. HELP!"

Ed read the note, nodded at Bill, bent over his paper, and began writing.

Dave looked around for a new partner, and he saw that Lynsey was passing notes with Helena. They seemed to be having a great time, nodding a lot and cracking each other up. *Probably gossiping,* he thought. *About something really stupid.*

He grabbed a clean sheet of paper and began a note to Lynsey: "What's the difference between you and a toxic waste dump?" But he decided that riddle was too harsh, even for Lynsey. Even if it *was* true.

He crumpled the paper and took another sheet.

But before he started writing, he got up, walked to a bookcase, and grabbed a dictionary.

He flipped the pages and then ran his fingers down a column of words. And there it was:

um also **umm** ([ə]m)
interjection. Used to express doubt or uncertainty or to fill a pause when hesitating in speaking.

So Lynsey had been right about something. For once.

He sat back down and wrote, "Hey, Captain Burgess, how's the war going? Ready to surrender?"

Dave nudged Jason, handed him the note, and pointed at Lynsey.

Jason nudged Lynsey and held the note out to her. And when she glared at him, Jason shook his head and pointed back at Dave.

Lynsey made a face and then took the paper, holding it between her thumb and forefinger like it was a squashed toad.

She read the message, wrote a little, and nudged Jason, who passed the paper back to Dave.

Her reply was, "It's <u>General</u> Burgess. Check the

score, dimbo. Girls rule, boys are losers. As usual. You're gonna get totally <u>schooled</u>!"

Jason handed the paper back to Dave. He read her message, made a snarly face at her, and then wrote, "Don't count on it. Always the big talker."

And sitting there frowning at the paper, once again Dave felt this overpowering wish that he could show Lynsey who was the boss, settle the question once and for all, really put her in her place.

And in answer to this wish, an idea popped into his head—an idea he probably should have ignored.

But he didn't.

Pressing down hard with his pencil, Dave wrote, "How about you and me go head-to-head, have our own special no-talking match? Starting right now, you and me. Unless you're scared. And the winner gets to write a big *L* on the loser's forehead. With permanent marker. On the playground after lunch on Thursday. How's <u>that</u> sound?" And he gave the paper to Jason.

Lynsey grabbed the paper from Jason and read it, and there was no hesitation. She looked at Dave, nodded a big yes, held up her hand with her fingers making an *L*, and pointed at him. Then she wrote something and handed the paper to Helena, who read everything, wrote something, and passed the paper back to Lynsey, who wrote something more and then passed the paper to Jason, who passed it back to Dave.

Lynsey had written, "Helena, you be the witness. Sign here." And Helena had written her name. And below Helena's signature, Lynsey had added, "No backing out now, fatmouth. Which color marker do you like best—red or black?"

Dave pointed at her and pretended to laugh and laugh. She stuck out her tongue and then turned away and picked up her chat with Helena.

Dave felt like he'd lost that skirmish. Lynsey always had a way of firing the last cannonball.

Then he smiled as he thought how much fun it would be to paint a big *L* on her forehead. If he could win, that is. Otherwise . . .

Dave wouldn't have put his feelings into these exact words, but he sat there in the quiet room sort of wishing it didn't have to be a war. Because it was . . . well, it was very *interesting*. Not talking was interesting all by itself, even without the extra fun of the contest. And the extra risk of his new private battle with Lynsey.

And he suddenly wondered what Lynsey thought about it, about the whole idea. And he wondered if she'd be honest enough to tell him.

So Dave grabbed a fresh sheet of paper and wrote, "I'm kinda glad we're all doing this—the no talking thing. Like, I really didn't know 'um' was a word. It's pretty interesting. At least it is to me." Then he gave the paper to Jason.

Jason tapped Lynsey's arm and handed her the new note. She read it and then gave Dave a short, suspicious look. And then she bent over the paper and wrote.

Jason handed him the paper, and Dave read her message. It said, "It is to me, too. I'm thinking and thinking and <u>thinking</u>. Pretty amazing."

Dave turned and caught Lynsey's eye, and they half nodded at each other. For one tiny fraction of a second, it wasn't boys against girls, and it wasn't a battle. It was two smart kids enjoying an idea.

Jason handed Dave another note, from him this time. "I'm <u>not</u> your personal delivery boy. Maybe you and Lynsey should sit at the same desk—ha ha ha!"

Dave's face felt hot. He scribbled "You're crazy!" onto Jason's note and jammed it back at him.

And at the bottom of the page he and Lynsey had passed, he wrote, "Yeah, but no way are you gonna win this fight. You and your stupid friends are going <u>down</u>, big-time!"

And as Dave tossed the note above Jason's head

so it landed on Lynsey's desk, he made an ugly face at her, and then shook his hands, like he was trying to flip something gross off his fingers.

He didn't wait for Lynsey's reaction. Dave turned away and began writing a new note. To Scott.

All during seventh period Mr. Burton sat at his desk, watching. He wrote some notes too, but they were notes to himself.

-No hesitation—everyone jumped
right in.
-Some frustration with writing—
it's slow.
-Some anger displayed.
-A lot of nodding and gesturing,
some hand signals.
-Tapping on desks and arms
and shoulders to get attention,
some poking, too.
-Mouth sounds—tongue clicking,
lip popping, raspberries.
-Some animal sounds—quacking,
whistling, barking, sometimes to
get attention, sometimes to
bother.

*—Not much boy-girl or girl-boy
note passing—but more than I'd
expected from this group.
—A lot of smiling and frowning
and other face-making
—Not one single word out loud!*

Mr. Burton was taking a class at the state university two nights a week, studying for his master's degree. The course was called Human Development, and one of the topics they had studied was the way children learn to use language.

Of course, this wasn't watching kids learn to *use* language. These students were already good with words. Almost too good.

No, this was watching children try to change how they expressed themselves, trying to use language in a new way.

Mr. Burton was pretty excited. It was like having his own private language lab. He thought, *If I keep careful notes, I bet I can write my big research paper on this! I can do interviews with the kids—once they start talking again. And I can gather information from the other teachers, too. There's so much good stuff to work with. This is great!*

When the last bell rang, Mr. Burton was sorry

the class had to end. And he couldn't wait for his first class on Wednesday morning.

For the fifth graders, that last bell on Tuesday meant something else.

It meant they had to go ride a bus. And not talk.

The bell meant they had to go to sports practice, or to dance or music lessons. And not talk.

It meant they had to go home and deal with moms and dads and brothers and sisters and neighbors and everyone else. And not talk.

No one was sure how all that was going to work, including Dave.

But Dave was absolutely sure of one thing: *He* was going to do everything just right. Because if he messed up, it meant he'd be walking around school on Thursday afternoon with a big *L* on his forehead.

And *that* was not going to happen.

CHAPTER 14

SEEN BUT NOT HEARD

The homebound school buses were quieter than usual on Tuesday afternoon, especially the ones hauling a large number of fifth-grade kids.

But none of the fifth graders found the ride home very hard. With no grown-ups around, it was pretty easy to keep quiet. A few of them sat with friends and passed notes back and forth. Some read books or opened a notebook and did homework. Most of the fifth graders just sat quietly—looking and listening. And thinking.

For the fifth graders like Lynsey who stayed for soccer or field hockey or cross-country, after school was just like regular school, because the coaches were all teachers, and you could answer teachers because of the three-word rule. Everyone was getting pretty good at that part of the contest.

Soccer practice was easy for Lynsey. Instead of yelling for the ball like she sometimes did, she just waved a hand or made a motion with her head. To direct teammates to cover an area or move downfield, she pointed. Lynsey was good at soccer. She did most of her communicating with her feet.

For the kids like Dave who went right home after school, not talking was more difficult. A *lot* more difficult. Because it's a fact of nature that parents don't like it when kids don't answer them.

"David?"

Dave had been home five minutes when he heard his mom come in the front door and call his name. He was upstairs. In the bathroom.

She called again. "David, answer me!"

To be more specific, Dave was sitting on the toilet.

"DAVID! ANSWER ME!"

Dave knew that tone of voice. He had to do something right away. So he reached over and banged on the inside of the bathroom door.

It was the wrong move.

His mom was up those front stairs and had both

hands on that locked bathroom doorknob in two seconds.

"David? Is that you? Are you all right? David? David! Answer me!"

She was going to kick down the door, Dave was sure of it.

He jiggled the doorknob, flushed the toilet, and was up and zipped and buttoned, all in about two seconds, and he yanked the door open and gave his mom the best smile he could manage.

Mrs. Packer was so relieved that she bent down and hugged Dave so hard that he couldn't have said a word even if he'd wanted to. Which he didn't.

But then she held him out in front of her and gave him a stern look. "Didn't you hear me calling you?"

It would have been easy to shake his head no and tell a silent lie, but Dave smiled and shrugged and held out his hands. Then he pointed at his mouth.

His mom frowned even more. "Your throat? Is your throat sore? Is that it?"

Dave shook his head.

"But it's hard to talk? Something hurts? Should I call Dr. O'Hara's office? We can drive right over there."

Dave shook his head again and motioned for his mom to follow him.

He went to his room, and then to his desk, and on a piece of paper he wrote, "Sorry. It's a thing we're doing at school. Not talking for a couple of days. That's all."

His mom looked at the paper. "Not talking?" she said. "Don't be silly. Everybody has to talk."

Dave smiled and shrugged. And he wrote, "Not all the time."

His mom tilted her head back and made a face at him, nodding slowly. "Ohhh . . . so you're saying that I talk all the time, is that it?"

Again, Dave smiled and shrugged.

"Because I could be as quiet as anybody." Then she added, "If I wanted to."

Bending over to pick up a sweatshirt, she pushed it into his arms and said, "Well, anyway, get the rest of these dirty clothes picked up and go downstairs and start a load in the washer. Only the dark colors, all right?"

Dave made a face, and she said, "And don't give me any of that sass, mister."

At his karate class Kyle did a front snap-kick—without a yell.

Mr. Hudson bowed and said, "Kyle-san. Always yell like this when you kick: Hii-*YAH*! Now you."

Kyle did the kick again, and he moved his face and mouth, but he didn't yell.

Mr. Hudson's face got red, and he walked stiffly like he always did when he was displeased. But he was still being polite, because that is the karate way.

He bowed. "Kyle-san. Did you not hear me?"

Ben Ellis walked onto the mat and bowed to Mr. Hudson. He was in fourth grade. When Mr. Hudson bowed back, Ben said, "Hudson-san. The fifth-grade kids aren't talking. None of them."

Hudson-san bowed and made a wise face and tried to imagine what the teacher in the movie *The Karate Kid* would say in this situation.

And after a long pause he said, "Ahh, I see. Yes. Silence. It is good."

Then he bowed at Kyle-san. And Kyle-san bowed back.

Then Kyle did another snap-kick. Without yelling.

Ellen played the first flute piece for her teacher, but there was a problem.

Mrs. Lenox said, "All right, we're in four/four time here." She used her pencil and pointed at a quarter rest. "How many beats of silence do you allow for this rest?"

Ellen tapped once on the music stand.

Her teacher said, "Correct, but just say, 'one beat.'"

Then Mrs. Lenox pointed at the symbol for a whole rest. "And how many beats for this one?"

Ellen tapped out four beats.

"Just say 'four beats,' dear."

Ellen smiled and tapped four times, and then pointed at her mouth and shook her head.

"What?" asked Mrs. Lenox.

Again Ellen pointed at her mouth and shook her head.

"Your lips? Something about your lips?" asked the teacher. "Just tell me, dear."

Ellen smiled and shook her head. Then she lifted the flute to her lips and played the piece again, and this time she read all the rests perfectly.

Her teacher nodded, smiled, and then turned the page to the next piece. Before Ellen began to play, Mrs. Lenox pointed at each rest, and Ellen tapped out the right number of beats. The teacher nodded, and Ellen began to play.

When she finished, Mrs. Lenox smiled, pointed at the start of the piece, picked up her own flute, nodded, and they played the whole piece again as a duet.

Neither of them said a word for the rest of the lesson.

• • •

Brian's mom picked him up at school, and when he got in the car, she said, "You need a haircut. We're stopping at Zeke's on the way home."

Brian groaned and shook his head. He stamped his feet on the floor of the car. His mom kept driving.

Brian hated going to Zeke's Modern Barbershop.

Zeke was this grumpy guy who'd been cutting hair in Laketon for more than forty years. He gave everyone the same haircut—short on top and buzzed close on the sides.

But the last two times he'd been there, Brian had forced Zeke to do a halfway decent job—but only because he practically yelled at the man the whole time. "Not so short on top. No, really, that's enough off the top. And don't use the clippers on the sides. Just scissors . . . there, that's enough. Don't cut off any more. Really. No, please, no clippers. Just use scissors. Please."

And that's why today was the wrong day for a haircut. If Zeke got him into that worn-out barber chair, Brian knew he'd end up looking like something that had escaped from the zoo.

When his mom parked the car, Brian jumped out and dashed into the pizza place next to the barber shop. But his mom followed him. He pointed at the menu, but she shook her head. "There's no time for a snack. We have to pick up your sister in fifteen minutes." She took him by the arm and pulled him out of the restaurant and over to Zeke's door. "Now get in there. Quick—there's no line right now."

Brian wanted to say, *News flash, Mom: There's never a line at Zeke's. The man's a rotten barber. And he has bad breath.*

But Brian couldn't say that. And he wouldn't be able to talk to Zeke, either. He was doomed.

Fifteen minutes later, when his big sister got into the car, she took one look at Brian and burst out laughing. She said, "Zeke, right?"

Brian could only nod. He had paid a heavy price for keeping his mouth shut. But he'd kept his promise to Dave and the other guys, and if they didn't beat the girls, well, it wasn't going to be his fault. And he had the bad haircut to prove it.

Was it worth it? *Yeah*, he thought, *it was worth it. So what if I look like a monkey for a week? Or two. Or three.*

Brian stared out the side window and tried not to think about it.

Mrs. Burgess was worried. She glanced in the rearview mirror and looked at her daughter's face again and thought, *Did she have a horrible day at school?*

Is that what's bothering her? Or maybe something hap-pened at soccer practice—that coach of hers can be pretty rough.

About a month earlier, Lynsey had started riding in the backseat of the car instead of up front. Her mom had noticed that her bright, chatty little girl was starting to become more serious, sort of distant now and then. And today? Not even a word, and barely a nod as she got into the car after practice.

Lynsey's mom thought, *Maybe she's giving me the silent treatment because I said she couldn't go to that sleep-over at Kelly's this weekend. That's probably it. Kids can be so moody sometimes—goodness knows I was!*

The truth is, Lynsey wasn't feeling moody at all. She was just thinking. Actually, she was thinking *about* thinking. Not talking all afternoon had made her realize something: For years now, she had done most of her thinking out loud. *I've been just blurting out whatever's on my mind—to my sister, to my mom—and at school? I just go on and on. And then I talk on the phone all night. Incredible!*

Lynsey hated to admit it, but Dave Packer might have been right about the top of her head explod-ing. Because that's how it had felt at first.

She felt like a faucet had been wide open, gush-ing and gushing forever, and then suddenly it flipped shut. And all her thoughts had been bottled up.

But by the time school let out, Lynsey had started to enjoy the change. And all during soccer practice, she'd felt like she was alone, just her and her own voice. And she'd felt like saying, *Hi there, I'm Lynsey—remember me? I live here.*

Thinking. And being quiet. It was different. And it was good.

As the car turned onto their street, almost home, she looked up and saw her mom's eyes in the car mirror, and instantly felt how worried she was. So Lynsey gave her mom a wave and a big smile. And her mom smiled back.

All over town, the other fifth graders were figuring out how to get along without talking. Were there any mistakes made on Tuesday afternoon? Yes, but only a few. Every single fifth-grade girl and boy was working hard not to talk.

And later on, as it got to be dinnertime and family time and homework time and bedtime, there were other problems the kids faced—a phone call from Grandma, a little brother who needed help with homework, a family trip to the mall for new shoes—lots of situations that begged for spoken words. Every single kid had unusual experiences Tuesday night, and every single kid had to be creative and alert . . . and quiet.

But it's not time to tell about all that.

It's time to go back to school, back in time to about three thirty on Tuesday afternoon, back to the conference room next to the office.

Because that's where the principal and the fifth-grade teachers had held a special meeting.

And they'd had *plenty* to talk about.

CHAPTER 15

CONTROL CENTER

"So. You've been with our fifth graders all afternoon. You've seen—and heard—what they're doing. What do you think should be done?"

Mrs. Hiatt looked from face to face around the conference table.

Mrs. Marlow spoke right up. "We should get them all in the auditorium tomorrow morning and lay down the law—just stop it. It's silly and it's disruptive. I mean, it's interesting, and all that. And with these kids, it's maybe even an improvement. But it's still not right. It was sort of cute right after lunch today, but then I had the second group, and then the third during seventh period. And by then it was just a bother, a real distraction. We've got a lot of material to cover in science. So I say we should squash the whole thing right away."

Mrs. Escobar nodded her agreement. "It's very

annoying in math class, these short answers they use. It's a game to them, and that's all they're paying attention to. I'm trying to work, and if they're playing a game, it's frustrating. Very frustrating. So if this is a vote, I say we stop it first thing tomorrow."

Mr. Burton shook his head. "But why? It's very inventive, what they're doing. And it's creative, and they're all thinking. And I think it's mostly positive, too. They're all exercising some self-control—which is a big change for this group. I think we should try to have a sense of humor about it, just let it run its course. It can't go on for very long, can it? What's the harm?"

"Well, it's not a problem in the gym," said Mrs. Henley. "Actually makes it easier, me not having to yell and all. I've got no complaints. If they want to be like they were this afternoon the whole rest of the year, it's perfectly fine by me."

"It's *not* fine by me." That was Mrs. Akers talking. "I only get them for music two or three times a week, and I need to make every minute count. And I asked Jim Torrey, and he feels the same way about art class. I went along with it this afternoon, and we had some fun, too. But I can't afford to waste more class time. I can't teach them songs if they won't sing more than three words in a row."

"I just realized something," said Mrs. Overby.

"You know what that little rascal Dave Packer did yesterday? Instead of giving an oral report, he stood up at the front of the class and coughed for two, maybe three whole minutes. And he was *pretending*, I'm sure of it. So he wouldn't have to talk! This really has to stop."

Mr. Burton said, "But don't you remember? We're talking about the Unshushables. These kids have been driving the whole school nuts for years and years. And suddenly, like some amazing gift from elementary school heaven, they all stop talking, and what are we going to do? We're going to start 'em right up again. That doesn't make sense. Why not wait a little? You know, see what happens. Just for another day or so. What's the harm in that?"

Mr. Burton honestly didn't think it was a problem. But even if he had, he would have asked the other teachers to back off anyway. He was hoping the quiet time would go on long enough for him to gather more information for that paper he needed to write for his Human Development class.

The principal had heard enough. She was glad to get everyone's opinion, but she didn't want the teachers turning against each other. This was *her* school, and like everything else, this decision was her responsibility.

Mrs. Hiatt said, "Thank you for your thoughts—very helpful. But this is not a voting situation. And I've made my decision. You know I've been trying to get these kids to quiet down ever since they were in first grade. So it's tempting to go along with this activity of theirs and hope it will lead to an improvement. But I think that would be wrong. The sudden quiet might seem easier than all the noise, but neither behavior is really what we want. These children need to learn to be quiet when it's right to be quiet, and they need to talk and participate at the right times too. We don't want an all-or-nothing situation—which is what this is. What we need is real balance, real self-control. If we let them keep up this game or contest or whatever it is, I think we'll be sending the wrong message. So we need to have an assembly tomorrow. I've noticed that Lynsey Burgess and Dave Packer seem to be the ringleaders. And I—"

"Actually," Mrs. Marlow interrupted, "I think it's more like Dave and Lynsey are sort of team captains. They're keeping score, counting words. And it's the boys against the girls. I intercepted a note."

The principal raised her eyebrows. "A note? You didn't tell me that."

Mrs. Marlow shrugged. "It was this afternoon. In my classroom."

Mrs. Hiatt said, "It might have been helpful if you'd told me about this sooner." The principal paused, letting everyone feel how displeased she was.

And in that moment, Mr. Burton thought, *Women—always keeping little secrets.*

But he immediately corrected that thought. Because anybody who hangs on to stereotypes about girls and boys . . . shouldn't. Especially if he's a teacher.

The principal said, "Anyway, that's good to know. And I think I see a way to approach the problem. So at the start of homeroom, please bring all the students to the auditorium."

It was quiet for a moment.

Then Mr. Burton said, "What are you going to do if the kids don't respond? To your approach."

Mrs. Hiatt looked at him, a trace of frost in her eyes. "What do you mean?"

"Well," he said, "I'm just saying that we've got five years of experience with this group. They've never obeyed very well when we've told them to stop being noisy. Why should it be any different when we tell them to stop being so quiet?"

Mrs. Hiatt stared at Mr. Burton a moment, and in her mind a little voice said, *Leave it to a man to say something negative.*

But, of course, she immediately corrected herself.

Because that kind of thought can get a principal in trouble. On a school faculty, it's never supposed to be girls against boys. In fact, that's called discrimination, which is against the law.

So Mrs. Hiatt looked around the table, smiled, and said, "All I can promise is that I'll do my best to resolve this situation in the most orderly way possible. And I know that each of you will do the same. See you all first thing in the morning."

As the teachers left the conference room, there wasn't much talking.

In fact, there was none.

CHAPTER 16

ORDERS

It was a bright November Wednesday, and the morning playground at Laketon Elementary School rang with the usual shouts and laughter of children.

But there was another layer of schoolyard activity going on—if a person knew what to look for. Because all around the swing sets and the jungle gym and the baseball diamonds, small groups formed up as fifth-grade friends passed notes and gestured and play-acted, trying to tell each other what had been happening since Tuesday after school; trying to tell each other all the clever ways they'd gotten along without talking. The fifth graders were so *glad* to see each other. They felt like they had spent Tuesday night in lonely prison cells, practically in solitary confinement.

There was also some contest business being

conducted. It was time for the first test of the overnight honor system. As agreed upon beforehand, boys who had spoken illegal words reported to Lynsey, and the girls reported to Dave.

As Dave received the morning confessions from a short line of sheepish girls, he felt pretty good. He added fifteen more points to the score against the girls.

Lynsey felt good too. By holding up fingers, four boys admitted that they'd spoken a total of twelve forbidden words—which seemed suspiciously low to her. But the rules were the rules, and she had to trust that the boys weren't lying—just like Dave had to trust the girls. And Lynsey admitted to herself that there might be a few cheaters on both sides. So it probably evened out. Anyway, she wasn't worried, because she was pretty sure that the girls were still winning.

When the first bell rang, everyone went inside.

Dave was in Mr. Burton's homeroom. When the second bell rang and all the kids sat silently at their desks, the teacher said, "Please line up at the door. We're going to a special fifth-grade assembly this morning. If anyone would like to guess what it's about, just speak up."

No one did, but Mr. Burton could tell from the

looks on their faces that most of them had a pretty good idea. He smiled and said, "But don't worry. Who could be upset with such beautifully behaved children? Not me, that's for sure."

After his group had filed into the auditorium and taken their seats, Dave turned and looked for Lynsey. She was sitting next to Kelly, and they were passing a note back and forth. She didn't look concerned at all.

Dave turned away quickly, so she wouldn't notice him looking at her. If Lynsey wasn't worried, he wasn't going to worry either—even though this assembly had to be about their contest. It *had* to be, didn't it? There had never been a special assembly at Laketon Elementary School before, at least not that he could remember.

And there had *certainly* never been an assembly that had begun in complete silence like this.

Lost in his thoughts, Dave didn't notice Mrs. Hiatt walking onto the stage. And she said something too, but he missed it.

Scott Vickers elbowed him in the ribs, and Dave snapped back to the present—just in time to see the principal looking right at him.

"Dave, I said I want you up here too."

In a daze, he looked around quickly and saw that Lynsey was already walking down the far aisle. So

Dave lurched to his feet, scooched past his class-mates, and hurried down the aisle and up the four steps onto the stage.

Mrs. Hiatt stood between them, and she said, "Now, as you know, students, we always begin an assembly with the Pledge of Allegiance. So, Lynsey, Dave, you will lead us in the Pledge this morning. Everyone, please stand up."

The whole fifth grade rose to their feet. In silence.

Dave glanced across at Lynsey, and she glanced at him. And the look they exchanged was clear: *What should we do?*

Lynsey gave a tiny shrug, and then they gave each other an even tinier nod. All of this happened in less than a second, and that's all it took for each to know that this was the right time for a temporary truce.

Dave and Lynsey looked out across the faces of their friends, nodded, put their right hands over their hearts, and turned to face the flag: signal sent, signal received.

These kids hadn't talked for more than eighteen hours. Every fifth grader took a deep breath, and if the pictures of Washington and Lincoln on either side of the stage had been painted with hands, they would have used those hands to cover their ears.

"I PLEDGE ALLEGIANCE TO THE FLAG
OF THE UNITED STATES OF AMERICA,
AND TO THE REPUBLIC
FOR WHICH IT STANDS,
ONE NATION, UNDER GOD, INDIVISIBLE,
WITH LIBERTY AND JUSTICE FOR ALL."

The kids spoke with one voice, almost shouting, incredibly loud, amazingly powerful—probably the most rousing Pledge of Allegiance ever heard in a public school during the entire history of the nation. The auditorium echoed, and it seemed to take a moment for the room to stop shaking.

As Dave and Lynsey hurried back to their seats, Mrs. Hiatt, her ears still ringing, said, "Thank you. That was . . . excellent. I have called this special fifth-grade assembly so that every one of you gets the same message at the same time. As of right *now*"—and here, the principal paused and swept her eyes over the upturned faces in front of her—"the contest, or game, or whatever you'd like to call this sudden quietness, or this three-words-in-a-row business you're all doing—as of right now, it's *over*. Ended. Stopped. It was interesting, and I hope you learned something, and we all hope that you also enjoyed yourselves. But I have decided that it needs

to stop. What you've been doing has made it very difficult to have normal, productive classroom activities. And, of course, that is why we're all here, to learn as much as we can every day. So, is that clear?"

The room was silent, and then a scattering of kids replied, "Yes, Mrs. Hiatt."

The principal said, "Is what I am saying clear to *everyone?*"

This time the whole group responded, "Yes, Mrs. Hiatt."

But there was no sudden rush of whispering, no undercurrent of talking in the auditorium, no joking and laughing—none of the usual behavior that the Unshushables were famous for.

The group remained silent.

And Mrs. Hiatt realized something: Yes, the kids had all responded to her, and just now they had all obediently said, "Yes, Mrs. Hiatt." But—that was only *three* words. And now it was still completely silent in the auditorium.

So, to really prove that they had actually *agreed* to behave normally, well . . . she would have to get them all to start talking . . . normally.

But the principal instantly decided that this did not feel like the right moment to push it. Better to let the teachers work it out with smaller groups, one class at a time.

So she smiled at the fifth graders and said, "Thank you for listening so carefully, and now I hope you all have a wonderful day. Teachers, you may take your first-period classes now."

Mrs. Hiatt watched the classes leave, one by one. It was a very orderly exit. All the kids were behaving extremely well.

But it didn't feel right. It was just too quiet.

CHAPTER 17

ALLIANCES

As he walked toward his first period class, Dave felt relieved. He was glad Mrs. Hiatt had put an end to the contest. He was especially glad that he wouldn't have to actually mark a big *L* on Lynsey's forehead. Or the reverse of that. Now he could just think about his schoolwork again. Because he really was a pretty good student. That's why he was in the high math group.

But as he went into the math room, he didn't talk to his friends, and they didn't talk to him. And none of the girls were talking either. No one was actually sure that the contest was over. And no one was taking chances. Including Dave.

The bell rang, and as everyone took their seats it was still completely quiet.

Mrs. Escobar got right down to business. "All right, students, we're still working on metric conversions, and, let's see . . . who's got an answer for the first home-work problem?"

Lynsey raised her hand, and when Mrs. Escobar nodded, she said, "Three hundred twelve."

Mrs. Escobar frowned. "'Three hundred twelve' what?"

Lynsey said, "Degrees Celsius."

Mrs. Escobar looked at Lynsey. "You heard what the principal said a few minutes ago?"

Lynsey nodded.

"About how this little game needs to stop?"

Lynsey nodded again, and then raised her hand.

Mrs. Escobar nodded, and Lynsey said, "But why?"

"Why?" said the teacher. "Because it's not good. For anyone. It slows down our classwork. Like right now. We should be doing math, and instead we're talking about . . . not talking."

Lynsey said, "Math is numbers."

"Yes," said Mrs. Escobar, "but we need to use words to talk about how we're using numbers. You know that. You all know that. So stop this. Right now."

Lynsey stood up and pointed at the dry erase board. "May I?"

Mrs. Escobar said, "Go ahead."

Lynsey had her homework paper in one hand and a marker in the other. She wrote out the numbers for the first problem and then showed the three steps she used to get the correct answer.

She turned to Mrs. Escobar, and when the teacher nodded, she said, "How's that?"

Mrs. Escobar was starting to boil over. "I am *not* amused by this, Lynsey. I know what you're doing, and I will *not* stand for it. Now *stop it!*"

Lynsey stood at the board. She pointed at the problem. "Is it right?"

Another three words.

Dave knew that look on the teacher's face. It meant trouble, serious trouble. And not just for Lynsey. He held his breath, waiting for the explosion.

But the very next moment, Dave amazed himself: He raised his hand.

Mrs. Escobar had to grit her teeth, but she managed to say, "Yes?"

Dave pointed at the solution on the board and said, "Mine is different."

Without asking permission, Dave was on his feet. He grabbed the marker from Lynsey and scrawled his work onto the board. He had the same answer, but he had worked with fractions instead of decimals.

Mrs. Escobar said, "How many of you did it the way Dave did?"

About half the hands went up.

"And the way Lynsey solved it?" The other half went up.

The teacher nodded. "That's good. Does everyone see why it can be done both ways?"

Everyone nodded.

"Okay, here's a tougher question: Kelly, which way was easier, Dave's way or Lynsey's way?"

Kelly said, "Lynsey's."

"Really?" asked the teacher. "How come?"

"Fewer steps."

And all around the room, Mrs. Escobar saw heads nodding, saw the special light that shows up on a kid's face when understanding happens.

She smiled. "That's right. Decimals really do make things easier."

Tyler raised his hand and said, "With a calculator." Which got a laugh from the whole class.

And as they laughed, Dave and Lynsey looked at each other for about half a second. Not quite a friendly look, but similar.

Then Dave thought, *This means the contest is still on*. And he wasn't sure how he felt about that.

The class sailed through the rest of the conversion

problems—miles to kilometers, kilograms to ounces, acres to hectares, on and on. And every student responded using three words or less, or with written answers on the board.

Mrs. Escobar knew the kids weren't obeying Mrs. Hiatt. She knew they were still counting words, still keeping silent unless called on.

But honestly, at this moment, she didn't care. She was in the middle of an amazingly productive class period—and everyone was so focused, so alert, so engaged. Compared to the classroom experience she'd had with these same kids just twenty-four hours ago, well, it was like night and day. And she liked the day much better.

And what was happening in the other first-period classrooms on Wednesday—classrooms where Lynsey and Dave were not on hand to provide some leadership?

As science class began, Mrs. Marlow had already decided to make an example of the first kid who gave her a three-word answer. And it happened to be Kyle.

"I *asked* you to tell me about the order Lepidoptera," the teacher said.

Kyle nodded. "Butterflies and moths," he repeated.

"And that's all you know?" she said.

He nodded again. "Pretty much." Which got a giggle from the class.

Mrs. Marlow grabbed a notepad and picked up a pencil, reading out loud as she wrote: "Dear Mrs. Hiatt, Kyle has refused to obey your instructions. He is not participating in class discussion, and he—"

Kyle raised his hand, and Mrs. Marlow snapped, "What?"

"I'm participating."

"No," she said, "you're *deliberately* using as few words as possible, and you are disobeying the principal."

Kyle shook his head. "I'm . . . conserving."

She said, "That's nonsense. Conservation means . . ."

Kyle finished the sentence: ". . . not wasting."

Mrs. Marlow glared at him. "Conservation is for energy and water and soil and forests. Words don't need conserving."

"Maybe they do," Kyle said, which was awfully brave of him.

And all the kids in the class nodded their agreement with Kyle. Which was also very brave.

Mrs. Marlow felt herself getting angry. However, she was an extremely logical person, and she had to admit that Kyle had a point. Anybody who had ever eaten lunch in the teachers' room or sat through a whole faculty meeting would have to agree that a *lot* of words get wasted every school day. And all that endless gabbing that had made the Unshushables so famous? Ninety-nine percent waste.

But she said, "Regardless of that, the principal said you must all participate *normally* in class."

Kyle scrunched up his face. "What's normal?"

Mrs. Marlow said, "In this case, it means talking the way the principal wants you to . . . the way I want you to . . . the way everyone usually talks and answers . . . normally."

Kyle said, "Can normal change?"

"Well . . . ," and Mrs. Marlow paused.

She paused because just three days ago they had discussed climate change, and she had explained how a normal high temperature *now* would have been considered *abnormal* a hundred years ago. And she knew Kyle would remember that. The whole class probably remembered. This was a very bright group.

She continued. "Yes, you could say that. But it's certainly not normal to use only three words at a time. Or no words at all. Not at school."

Kyle shrugged. "Works for me."

Mrs. Marlow thought back to all the times in the past week when she'd had to yell at Kyle about his nonstop whispering, about his constant joke-telling, about his never-ending comments on anything and everything that ran through his twitchy little head. And she looked at Kyle sitting there quietly, giving her his full attention. And every other student was doing the same thing.

And suddenly, the idea of trying to *make* these kids talk, actually *demanding* that they all go back to being noisy, self-absorbed chatterbrains—it simply wasn't . . . logical.

So Mrs. Marlow decided to go ahead with her lesson for the day, and she adjusted herself to the new normal. Because the *new* normal was at least ten times better than the *old* normal.

In social studies there were more oral reports, and Mrs. Overby called on Ed Kanner and Bill Harkness to go first.

The boys walked to the front of the room, stood shoulder to shoulder, and both of them looked down at the index cards in Bill's hands.

Ed said, "Italy is old."

Then Bill said, "The Roman Empire . . ."

And Ed said, "Ruled the world . . ."

And Bill said, "For many centuries."

And Mrs. Overby said, "*What* do you two boys think you're doing?"

Ed said, "Giving our report."

And Bill said, "On Italy."

"No," said the teacher, "you're still playing that game, counting the words."

"But we practiced," Ed said.

"We're ready," Bill said.

And Ed said, "Can we finish?"

Like the other teachers up and down the fifth-grade hall, Mrs. Overby had to make a decision: Go with the flow—which promised to be very quiet and orderly—or call for the principal, raise a ruckus, and try to force these kids to be their regular old noisy selves again.

As a student of history, Mrs. Overby knew about the power of a grassroots movement. She also knew about the power of civil disobedience.

But mostly, she decided that this no-talking craze was actually a pretty good social experiment. Plus, she didn't feel like the kids thought they were winning and she was losing—it wasn't like that. They were just having a different kind of communication experience—together. That's all.

True, Ed and Bill's report on Italy was choppy

and awkward and a little hard to follow as they passed the narration back and forth like a Ping-Pong ball. But the boys made all their points, learning took place, and the whole class sat silently and paid close attention. And the next five reports went almost as smoothly. What more could a social studies teacher ask for?

So, like the other teachers, Mrs. Overby chose the quiet way.

And she decided she'd talk to the other teachers later in the morning and see how they were handling this thing. And she'd talk to Mrs. Hiatt, too.

Language arts was the easiest class for the kids. Mr. Burton didn't even try to make them stop their "activity." If they wanted to be quiet and talk only in three-word bursts, he was all for it, no matter what the mighty Mrs. Hiatt had said. After all, this was his classroom, wasn't it? And if he believed this way of using words could provide a good language arts learning experience, then couldn't he proceed with it? Yes. Absolutely.

But he wasn't foolish. He walked to the back of the room, stuck his head out into the hallway, looked both ways, and then closed his door.

Back at the front of his room, Mr. Burton said,

"Eric and Rachel, please come up and sit in these chairs."

When they were seated, he said, "You two are going to have a short debate. A debate is an orderly argument, and each of you will take opposite sides on the same issue. And the question is, 'Should there be soft-drink machines in school cafeterias?' Rachel, you will argue *for* this question, and Eric, you will argue *against* it. You will take turns speaking . . . *and* you may use no more than three words for each statement. Ready?"

Eric and Rachel shook their heads no.

Mr. Burton said, "Don't worry. You'll both do fine. Eric, you first. And, you may begin."

Eric said, "Soft drinks . . . bad."

Rachel shook her head and said, "Not bad. Delicious."

Eric frowned. "Too much sugar."

Rachel said, "I like sugar."

Eric shook his head. "Sugar rots teeth."

Rachel smiled a big smile. "Not mine."

Eric said, "Milk is better."

Rachel shrugged. "Try sugar-free."

Eric said, "Still, bad . . . nutrition."

Rachel held up her arm and made a muscle. "I eat vegetables."

Eric said, "Not everyone does."

Rachel said, "I like choosing."

Eric said, "Soda is . . . expensive."

Rachel pulled a dollar from her pocket. "I have enough."

Eric said, "Spend it smarter."

Rachel said, "What about freedom?"

Eric shook his head. "Not at school."

Rachel smirked. "Very bad news!"

And they went on like that for about five minutes with no letup.

All the kids were fascinated, and, of course, so was Mr. Burton.

He took furious notes, writing down each response, trying to record the kind of gestures the kids made, their facial expressions, their tones of voice.

Very few words were being exchanged, but whole worlds of ideas were floating around as the kids tried to build their arguments. They got emotional, and the three-word limit was clearly a problem. Still, they packed a lot into so few words. It was like debating with condensed haiku.

It was also sort of like listening to cave people talk, or maybe Tarzan—"Hungry, eat now." And Mr. Burton wrote some three-word chunks of his own, which he intended to use in his Human Development paper:

-Every word counts.
-Choose power words.
-Hemingway would approve.
-Focus and narrow.
-Ideas are collapsible.
-Remember Miles Davis.

And as he looked at what he wrote, he thought, *Maybe I should write my whole paper using three-word sentences. That would certainly get the attention of my professor!*

In music class, the kids entered the room and sat silently, just like yesterday afternoon. Mrs. Akers was sure the students were going to disobey Mrs. Hiatt's orders, and she was ready to take some drastic steps to stop this nonsense.

But when she played an introduction and launched into "Over the River and Through the Woods," everyone sang right out.

The teacher was amazed. Mrs. Akers felt like there had been a glorious victory for the forces of law and authority, and she intended to write the principal a special note to say thanks for her strong leadership.

In fact, though, the principal's talk was *not* the direct cause of the singing.

Taron had written a simple note, and she'd shown it to all the boys and girls as they came into the music room:

Singing is <u>not</u> talking. Deal?

And by nodding, all the boys and all the girls had silently agreed that bending the contest rules a little was a good idea. Besides, no one wanted the Thanksgiving music program to sound lousy, and their contest would be over by then, anyway.

The boys and girls in that first-period music class might not have noticed it, but the important thing was not that they had agreed to sing. The important thing was that they had *agreed*. About anything. Fifth-grade boys and fifth-grade girls at Laketon Elementary School were actually cooperating and helping each other.

And that's what was happening in the other fifth-grade classrooms too. The boys and girls had joined forces without even realizing it. Together, they had resisted the pressure from the principal and from their teachers. They had used their wits and teamed up to prove that not talking was a simple, harmless activity. It wasn't like the boys and girls were getting all buddy-buddy or anything, and it wasn't like the teasing and taunting had completely stopped. Because old habits are hard to break.

But still, cooties were dying all over the place.

That was one result.

Another result of the morning classes was that the kids had won a new kind of respect from their teachers. Teachers have great respect for order and self-discipline. Teachers love to make careful plans and then put them into action—it's what they do. And teachers hate noise and disorder and bouncing kids, because these things keep them from accomplishing their careful plans.

However, there was one gigantic problem with all this harmony and order and balance and peace that was blooming in the fifth-grade hall: Mrs. Hiatt wasn't in the loop. She was clueless about these new developments.

In fact, the principal wasn't even in the building during the morning. She was across town at the district offices working on next year's budget. She had left her trusty teachers to carry out her strict orders.

But Mrs. Hiatt had organized her meetings to be sure that she would be back at her school in time for fifth-grade lunch. Because the principal felt sure she would be needed at lunch. With her bullhorn. To keep law and order, just like always.

Because Mrs. Hiatt had complete confidence in her teachers.

She was sure that by lunchtime everything would be back to . . . normal.

CHAPTER 18

ADVENTURES IN
THE RED ZONE

M rs. Hiatt got back to her school at 11:59. There were several messages on her desk, and Mrs. Overby had taped a note on her chair that read, "Please come see me in the teachers' room."

But the principal was in a hurry. She needed to be on time for fifth-grade lunch.

Five minutes later, for the second day in a row, Mrs. Hiatt found herself standing in the middle of a silent cafeteria holding a big red plastic bullhorn.

But today, it was different.

She looked around the quiet room, and the sight of all these fifth graders *deliberately* disobeying her— well, it nudged her over the edge. It pushed her right into the red zone.

She gritted her teeth, and an angry haze filled her mind, and she knew she was angry, and she knew it wasn't good to be angry. But she was.

And she knew it wasn't good to be angry and try to talk to children at the same time.

But she couldn't help herself. She *had* to talk to these kids. Right now.

She could have whispered, and every fifth grader would have heard her. But she didn't whisper.

She pulled the trigger on the bullhorn.

"HAVE YOU FORGOTTEN OUR ASSEMBLY THIS MORNING?"

The principal's voice echoed off the walls.

The kids stared at her.

She aimed the bullhorn at Dave and yelled, **"DAVID PACKER, ANSWER ME: DO YOU REMEMBER WHAT I TOLD ALL OF YOU THIS MORNING?"**

When Dave nodded his head, she yelled, ***"ANSWER* ME. WITH YOUR *VOICE*. OUT LOUD."**

So Dave swallowed his first bite of macaroni and cheese and said, "I remember." His voice sounded very small. Dave felt like he was the Scarecrow talking to the Great and Powerful Oz.

Mrs. Hiatt took five steps closer to Dave and

shouted, **"THEN WHY AREN'T YOU TALK-ING WITH YOUR FRIENDS?"**

Dave had never seen Mrs. Hiatt this mad before. And no one had ever yelled at him with a bullhorn. It seemed unfair. To be yelled at with that giant voice. So he decided he wasn't going to be afraid. Or angry. No matter what.

Dave shrugged and said, "Nothing to say."

Which was perfectly true. Before Mrs. Hiatt had started yelling, he had been very happy to just sit and eat and think.

"STAND UP!"

Dave stood up. Every kid in the room was watching him. And so was Mrs. Marlow. And the custodian. And the cafeteria workers.

Mrs. Hiatt said, **"TALK. I WANT YOU TO TALK RIGHT NOW. I WANT TO HEAR YOU TELL TODD EVERYTHING YOU LEARNED IN ALL YOUR CLASSES THIS MORNING. START TALKING TO TODD. NOW."**

Dave wasn't an angry sort of kid. Not usually.

In fact, there was only one thing that nudged him over the edge: being bullied. The only time he'd ever gotten into a fight at school was back in second grade when a fifth grader had started picking on him. That's when Dave had learned that you can't just go along with a bully. Because then you get bullied more and more.

And that's how Dave felt. Right now. He was getting mad. It felt like Mrs. Hiatt was being a bully—a bully with a bullhorn.

Again the principal yelled, **"TALK!"**

And that did it. It was Dave's turn for a trip to the red zone.

He glared at Mrs. Hiatt, and he shouted, "I do *not* have to talk now if I don't want to. This is *our* lunch time. *None* of us have to talk!"

And a sentence flashed into Dave's mind, something he had heard dozens of times on TV shows. This sentence was usually being said to criminals wearing handcuffs, but that didn't seem to matter at the moment.

Dave looked around the cafeteria at his classmates, and he shouted, *"You have the right to remain silent!"*

And with that, Dave pressed his lips together, folded his arms across his chest, and sat down.

Lynsey was the first to pick up on Dave's body language. She looked at Mrs. Hiatt and slowly folded her arms. All the girls at her lunch table did the same.

And the gesture spread through the room like

ripples on a pond. Every kid stared at the principal, arms folded and stone silent.

Mrs. Hiatt looked around slowly, drew herself up to her full height, and then walked briskly out of the room. She walked down the hall to the school office. She nodded at Mrs. Chaplin, the school secretary, and said, "Hold my calls." Then she went into her own office and closed the door.

Back in the cafeteria, it was dead calm. Every kid sat motionless, arms still folded, not sure what to do next.

Todd started it.

He unfolded his arms and nodded at Dave, and then he clapped his hands. In three seconds every fifth-grade boy was clapping like mad.

Dave looked around at his friends and smiled and nodded.

And a second later, guess who joined in? That's right: all the girls.

And five seconds later, the hooting and the whooping began.

It was loud in that cafeteria. It was *incredibly* loud.

The clapping and cheering was so loud that the sound went right through the cafeteria doors and walls and thundered down the hall—all the way to the school office, and right through the closed door of Mrs. Abigail Hiatt, principal.

The phone on Mrs. Chaplin's desk buzzed—an intercom call.

"Yes?" she answered. The secretary listened, nodded, and said, "Right away."

She got up and walked out of the office and down the hall and into the cafeteria, where it had gotten quiet again.

Mrs. Marlow was standing near the doorway, and Mrs. Chaplin whispered something to her.

Mrs. Marlow nodded and quickly walked halfway across the room.

She bent down close to Dave Packer's ear and said, "To the office."

Dave swallowed his third bite of macaroni and cheese and looked up into the science teacher's face. "I have to?"

She nodded, "Principal's orders."

Dave looked around the table at his friends. No one needed to speak a word—their faces said it all. And the message?

Three simple words, and Dave believed them: "You are *dead*!"

CHAPTER 19

APOLOGIES

There were two hundred and twenty-seven green tile squares on the hallway floor between the cafeteria and the school office. Dave counted each one to keep from thinking about what was going to happen next. But he thought about it anyway.

Mrs. Chaplin pointed at the principal's door. "Go right in."

Dave knocked. He knew he didn't have to, but it bought him another two seconds of delay.

Mrs. Hiatt said, "Come in," and Dave thought, *At least she's not using her bullhorn.*

He opened the door, and she was standing with her back to him, looking out the windows into the school courtyard.

Dave blurted out, "I'm sorry," and he said that because he knew he shouldn't have yelled at the

principal, even if he had been right. Which he still believed he was. He also apologized because he hoped it might help save his life.

Mrs. Hiatt turned around, and Dave was shocked to see the look on her face. Because she wasn't mad. She almost looked like she'd been crying, and her nose was pink.

She shook her head. "That's why I sent for you, so *I* could say that. I'm the one who got angry. And I yelled first, and I set a terrible example. So I hope *you'll forgive me.*"

Dave couldn't remember the last time a grown-up had apologized to him. And to have the *principal* saying she was sorry, well, he could barely manage a nod at her.

She nodded back, and then paused and said, "So, what are we going to do about this . . . situation?"

"Um . . . not sure," Dave said.

She frowned. "Please, you can talk freely in here. None of your friends can hear us."

Dave shook his head. "Honor system."

Mrs. Hiatt's eyebrows went up. "Oh? Of course. Very admirable. Well, maybe you can answer some questions for me, just to get started."

Dave said, "Sure."

"First of all, how did all this get going? Who started it?"

Dave smiled. "Mahatma Gandhi."

"Pardon me?" Mrs. Hiatt said.

Dave said, "He stopped talking."

The principal said, "And someone wanted to try that here, at school, right?"

Dave nodded, and pointed at himself. "All my fault."

"I see," she said. "How did you learn about Gandhi?"

He said, "Social studies report."

"And why did he stop talking?"

Dave shrugged. "To think more."

"But you're not keeping *silent*, not totally—why?"

Dave thought a moment and then said, "Respect. For school," which he knew was going to make him sound like a goody-goody. But it was true. He and his friends weren't trying to shut down the school. Not at all.

Mrs. Hiatt nodded slowly and said, "Oh."

She seemed to be out of questions.

And during that three or four seconds of silence, an idea jumped into Dave's mind—but he pushed it out. It was too outrageous.

But the idea bounced back into his head, and this

time Dave just blurted it out. "Want to join?"

Mrs. Hiatt bunched her eyebrows together. "What do you mean?"

"Join—stop talking."

She looked at Dave as if he had just told her to put on a grass skirt and dance the hula on the roof of a school bus. "Don't be silly—I'm the *principal*. Do you have any idea how many people I have to speak to? Every single day?"

Dave pointed at a notepad on her desk.

"May I?"

She nodded, and he wrote, "You can say only three words in a row. And only if a teacher or a grown-up talks to you first. Except you can talk to a kid first. Because you're sort of a teacher. And no talking at all outside of school—honor system. And the whole thing's almost over anyway—just until tomorrow."

Then Dave smiled up at her and said, "It's . . . interesting."

Mrs. Hiatt shook her head. "I could never—"

Dave put up his hand like a traffic officer: "There! Stop: three."

Mrs. Hiatt smiled—and it wasn't a principal smile. Dave could tell. She was smiling a real person smile.

She smiled because she realized Dave had offered her something important. Just five minutes earlier she had acted like—like a monster. But she wasn't, not really.

Still, she *had* behaved terribly. Everyone in the cafeteria knew that, kids and grown-ups both. And news like that spreads quickly. So somehow she needed to remind everyone that she *wasn't* a monster—fast.

And Dave had just offered her a way to become human again. Because it's a well-known fact that monsters do *not* have a sense of humor.

She tore Dave's sheet off the notepad, bent over the desk, and did some writing of her own.

She stepped quickly into the office and handed Mrs. Chaplin the paper.

The secretary read it over quickly and said, "And I should . . ."

The principal held up one finger and said, "Type." Then she held up two fingers and said, "Duplicate." And then she held up three fingers and said, "Distribute."

And Mrs. Chaplin said, "Got it."

Then, turning to Dave, the principal said, "Ready, set, go."

Dave's head was spinning, but he managed to say, "Where?"

She was already out the office door, and over her shoulder Mrs. Hiatt said, "To the cafeteria."

CHAPTER 20

THE WINNERS

At this point, it might be fun to tell how Dave followed the principal back to the cafeteria, and how Mrs. Hiatt apologized to the whole fifth grade—by trading three-word phrases back and forth with Dave. Who also apologized.

And describing the looks on the faces of all those fifth graders in the cafeteria, not to mention Mrs. Marlow and the rest of the staff—that might be fun too.

Or it might be interesting to tell how Mrs. Hiatt called an all-school assembly five minutes later by chiming the school intercom and then saying, "Everyone: auditorium. Hurry!" And how all the teachers in every grade were given five minutes at the assembly to explain the new no-talking rules to their students, and how loud and confusing it was as they did that; and then how completely quiet it got when the principal announced, "Silence starts . . . NOW!"

And it might be enlightening to explain how Mrs. Hiatt had changed the contest, so that the kids in kindergarten through fourth were competing grade against grade to see who could say the fewest illegal words during the next twenty-three hours— and why she thought her way was a better idea than boys against girls.

And it might be thought-provoking to explain how Dave felt about all this—how he felt that he was sort of like Gandhi, and how Mrs. Hiatt was sort of like the British Empire, and how he felt like there had been a great victory, "with liberty and justice for all"—which included Mrs. Hiatt herself.

And Mr. Burton—there's a lot that could be told about him, because he went completely stratospheric. He spent the last twenty-four hours of the contest scribbling down notes, taking photos, and using a little handheld recorder to capture as many three-word sentences as possible. He collected so much great material that he began thinking that he could not only write that paper for his Human Development course, he could practically write a whole *book* about the way the kids and teachers at Laketon Elementary School had changed the way they expressed themselves, changed their view of language itself—what it is, and how it works, and how communication can take so many different forms.

And speaking of human development, it might be fun to explore why the very youngest kids could not even *imagine* how to go without something as amazing and powerful as talking, not even for ten minutes—which is why the whole kindergarten was immediately excused from the activity.

And how about Thursday morning—when the boys reported zero honor system word-goofs and the girls reported only one? Telling how Dave and Lynsey reacted to *that* news would be revealing.

And then it would certainly be fun to peek at the challenges Mrs. Hiatt faced as she kept to a strict diet of three words at a time. On Wednesday afternoon, and again on Thursday morning, she talked with parents, with the superintendent, with the principals of other schools, with the electrician who arrived to repair the milk cooler, and, of course, with her teachers and with hundreds of kids—all of whom thought it was great to have a principal who just might be a little bit crazy.

In fact, the story could jump a whole week ahead, or even months ahead to see the way the fifth graders completed the school year as kinder, more careful talkers. And thinkers.

Because there's absolutely more to tell. There's *always* more.

But, as tempting as it is, it's not the time to tell about all that. Because this is the time to jump right to fifth-grade lunch on Thursday, right to that point when the *original* contest was coming to an end, right to that moment of truth when the boys and the girls were getting ready to compare their final scores.

Because with all the goodwill and the happy vibes that swirled out of Mrs. Hiatt's change of heart, plus the excitement of having the whole school go quiet, you might think that somehow the fifth-grade boys-against-girls contest didn't matter anymore.

But it did.

Remember when Dave stood up and shouted at the principal on Wednesday? Did you think no one was counting? Not true: *Everyone* was counting. Dave had said thirty words—grand words, brave and true. *However* . . . all but three of them were illegal.

At 12:14, one minute before the end of the contest, the cafeteria was silent. Every fifth grader was watching the second hand on the big clock. And so were all the fifth-grade teachers. And Mrs. Hiatt. And the custodian. And the school secretary, and the school nurse, too. No one wanted to miss this moment in the history of the Unshushables.

Dave and Lynsey sat across from each other at the same lunch table, ready for the big tally. Dave dug around in his back pocket and found the crumpled sheet listing all the points against the girls. And Lynsey pulled her little red notebook and a pencil out of her backpack, and she bent over it, adding and scribbling away.

Glancing down, Dave saw something poking out of the top pouch of Lynsey's backpack: a huge permanent marker, a red one.

And Dave had no trouble at all imagining a big L on his forehead. Because he already knew the final scores for both teams, and he was sure Lynsey did too.

With just fifteen seconds to go in the silent cafeteria, Lynsey stood up, looked down at the red notebook, took a deep breath, and—she talked. "I have to say this. My whole opinion changed. About boys. You really did the honor system great. And being quiet? Also great, everyone together. So . . . thanks."

And then the second hand pointed straight up,

and it was twelve fifteen, and the contest was over.

A yell went up that nearly peeled the tiles off the floor. Kids jumped out of their seats and ran and stood bouncing face-to-face with groups of friends, and everyone jabbered faster and louder than human beings ever should, laughing and nodding and telling everybody *everything* they were thinking and feeling.

And the louder it got, the louder everyone had to talk to be heard above the rising tumult, and the sound spiraled up toward that point where dogs run and stick their heads under a sofa.

And amid the burst of joy and noise and confusion, Lynsey shouted to Dave, "What's the official count?"

Dave nodded, cupped his hands around his mouth, and bellowed, "Forty-seven. Against the girls."

Lynsey looked at her notebook. She didn't try to talk—it was too loud for that. She turned the notebook around, and at the bottom of the page a number was circled. Seventy-four against the boys—a huge defeat.

Lynsey gave him an odd little smile, and Dave was ready for the teasing to begin. She shouted, "You didn't count?"

He was confused. "Count? Count what?"

Lynsey yelled as loud she could. "What I said, at the end."

Dave shook his head. "What?" The sound around them was deafening.

Lynsey flipped a page, and then turned the red notebook around so Dave could see it. And there was her whole little speech, written out word for word. The last word was "thanks," and above it she'd written a number: twenty-seven.

Dave nodded slowly as he stared at the speech and saw what Lynsey had done. He did the math in his head . . . *seven plus seven, and carry the one* . . . She had made the contest an exact tie—seventy-four points for each team.

And their private war? To see who got to label the other a loser?

Also a tie—her twenty-seven words matched the illegal ones he had yelled at Mrs. Hiatt.

Was it all too perfect? Of course it was. Had Lynsey messed with the score against the boys to make it add up that way? Without a doubt. Would there be a big investigation? Not likely.

Dave kept looking at the notebook. Lynsey's speech was filled with cross-outs and changes. She'd chosen those last words so carefully, making each one count.

He wanted to say, "I owe you, big-time."

He also wanted to say, "I guess I'm pretty much of an idiot, aren't I?"

And most of all, he wanted to say what she'd already said: "Thanks."

But Dave and Lynsey just sat there grinning at each other in the noisy cafeteria, and neither of them said a thing.

Not one word.

Andrew Clements was born in Camden, New Jersey. After receiving a B.A. in English literature and an M.A. in elementary education, he taught in the public schools north of Chicago for seven years—fourth grade, eighth-grade English, and high school English—and then he moved to New York, where he began working in the publishing business.

Mr. Clements's first book was published in 1985. Five years later, in 1990, he began writing a story about a boy who makes up a new world. The enormous success of *Frindle* had the eventual effect of turning Mr. Clements into a full-time writer.

Andrew Clements has written more than fifty books for children, including *The Last Holiday Concert*, *The Report Card*, and the *New York Times* bestseller *Lunch Money*. He has four grown children and lives with his wife in central Massachusetts.

Brian Selznick grew up in suburban New Jersey. The art programs in the public schools that Brian attended were very good, and he soon found himself in college at the Rhode Island School of Design. His first book, *The Houdini Box*, won the Texas Bluebonnet Award and the Rhode Island Children's Book Award. *When Marian Sang*, by Pam Muñoz Ryan, received the 2003 Orbis Pictus Award for outstanding nonfiction for children; and *The Dinosaurs of Waterhouse Hawkins*, by Barbara Kerley, was named a 2002 Caldecott Honor Book. Brian won the 2008 Caldecott Medal for *The Invention of Hugo Cabret*. Brian's other books include *The Doll People* and *The Meanest Doll in the World*, both by Ann M. Martin and Laura Godwin, and *Our House*, by Pam Conrad.

Brian is proud of his long collaboration with Andrew Clements, which began with *Frindle* and has gone on to include *The Landry News*, *The School Story*, and *Lunch Money*, as well as the covers for many of Clements's other books.

Mark Elliott is the illustrator of many picture books and novels for young readers, including the recent *Dexter the Tough* by Margaret Peterson Haddix. As a child he would tape together shirt boards to draw dinosaurs life-size. He currently resides at comfy Heron Hollow in New York's Hudson River Valley.

GREAT MIDDLE-GRADE FICTION FROM
Andrew Clements,
MASTER OF THE SCHOOL STORY

FRINDLE
0-689-80669-8
(hardcover)

0-689-81876-9
(paperback)

THE SCHOOL STORY
0-689-82594-3
(hardcover)

0-689-85186-3
(paperback)

THE LANDRY NEWS
0-689-81817-3
(hardcover)

0-689-82868-3
(paperback)

ROOM ONE
0-689-86686-0
(hardcover)

0-689-86687-9
(paperback)

THE JANITOR'S BOY
0-689-81818-1
(hardcover)

0-689-83585-X
(paperback)

A WEEK IN THE WOODS
0-689-82596-X
(hardcover)

0-689-85802-7
(paperback)

"Few contemporary writers portray the public school world better than Clements."—*New York Times Book Review*

www.SimonSaysKids.com